CHIMERA

Four Stories and a Novelette

JULIAN MIHDI

Raju,
May we find
endless love on
our path of
harmony ♡

Julian
Mihdi

Chimera

Published by On-Demand Publishing, LLC. 2017

Scotts Valley, CA, USA

First Printing, 2017

ISBN 978-0998713229

Cover art by Nicolas Aurelio Luna Fleck: www.nicolaslunafleck.com

*"Do not be bewildered by surfaces;
in the depths all becomes law."*
~Rainer Marie Rilke~

Table of Contents

CHIMERA

Foreword

❦

Although it is possible to trace her back to Egyptian antiquity, we first learn of the fire-breathing Chimera by way of Homer in *The Iliad*. Said to have lived in the land of Lycia, the beast is described as "a lion in front, a snake behind, and in between a goat." Of its exploits we cannot say much, except that the formidable creature was slain by the archer Bellerophon astride an airborne Pegasus (much to the relief of all Lycians, we can imagine). In the *Aeneid*, however, Virgil claims that the Chimera can still be found guarding the gates of Hades "armed with flame".

Scholars' credulity towards the Chimera began to wane, however, to the point where we find Cicero, the Roman rhetorician, scoffing, "Who believes…that the Chimera ever existed? The years obliterate the inventions of the imagination, but confirm the judgments of nature." Homer's tripartite beast gradually fell out of favor, becoming less a symbol of terror and more one of human fabrication. This transition is enshrined in the modern term "chimerical", commonly defined as something illusory or improbable.

The reader will be quick to notice that no snake-tailed, Lycian monsters populate this collection of stories. The strange incidents of mythology are often expropriated for the sake of metaphor, and this writer has only bowed to literary tradition in doing so. In assessing our post-modern world, fraught with hypocrisy, suffering and confusion, it is reasonable to speculate that humanity has set loose a hybridized beast of his own making. Having chosen a descent into the underworlds of ego, we are now confronted by the fury of our living experiment, with seemingly no Pegasus to lift us skyward.

There are countless threads that comprise our chimerical reality, public and personal, universal and individualized. Our outer environment mysteriously conforms to our inner lives, and so it is that every organ of mankind is in uproar. The Chimera of today's worldly experience is but a probability actualized, its various and bizarre features molded into being by irresponsible imagination. That man can create a means whereby his own spirit and vitality are constantly denigrated is the most terrifying of ironies—yet it also indicates, with a kind of winking humor, how easily the potential of his salvation might be won.

Our actions are fated to echo persistently in the worthy minds of our descendants; our character, too, will be recorded in the Book of Life without scruple or amendment. If we are only a glimmer in the cosmic Eye, the light remains sufficient to electrify the remainder of our history. Self-deception is the anesthetic that leads us to common forgetfulness. Banishing the Chimera could be as simple as **remembering**. We already hold the fateful arrow at our side—it's only a matter of pulling back the string, without fear.

—Salt Lake City, 2017

For Jack Korte

CHIMERA

Shedd Wilson, Antiques

AMr. Shedd Wilson of Goldsberry Lane in Athens, Georgia distractedly probed his teeth with a toothpick after lunch. The sun was high and a mayonnaise stain blotched his otherwise pristine khakis. Mr. Wilson was, of course, unaware of both realities. But perhaps he can be excused, for far more urgent matters turned the gears of his attention. As many suspect when they have reached the so-called twilight of their life, Mr. Wilson had had, he believed, enough of those quiet raptures in a well-lived life to sustain an engaging autobiography. No, he had never written a book before—he had always been too occupied with his antique shop for that. Further, it had occurred to Mr. Wilson that, in the constant presence of so many thick-bound, dusty atlases and impenetrable tomes, any sort of "book" on his part would be a petty superfluity—rather like an independently-owned coffee shop that crops up near a new, sprawling mall complex in the hopes of capturing (like a Venus fly-trap) some stray customers.

But Mr. Wilson had irritably shooed away this conception amid a mounting conviction that, yes, his life did have meaning after all. Not only that, he intoned inwardly, but it also contained those sudden intrigues that made experience go this way or that, the U-turns and sharp rights which, by fate's hand, map out the path of a resilient hero. Never mind that Mr. Wilson's profession camouflaged him in the anonymity of the past and rendered him a (questionably) living relic among many moth-ball-laden ones, or that the members of living society regarded him, like his shop's contents, as an object of passing interest—(enough of this) no, there was something greater, deeper, more true to the stupendous animation of the world in the life of Shedd Wilson, something more than the name on his bleary shopfront sign could ever convey, that nevertheless *should* be conveyed.

Yes, there had been Elaine in her summer dresses of brightening youth, and that one trip to blazing Egypt and Morocco on the business of inquiring into the availability of some rare amulets—he had wound up losing his passport and, subsequently, most of his marbles, but nevertheless had become enamored of weighty street falafels. (Now noticing the drying mayonnaise stain on his khakis, cursing his Dixie-bred cravings) On that autumn day of Elaine's funeral, ten years ago, Mr. Wilson ate salty finger food with slices of cheese, nodding quietly, deferentially as the townspeople offered their condolences around the limey red punch bowl. It occurred to many as they left the graveyard that crimson-shaded afternoon that, indeed, Mr. Wilson seemed equipped quite ably for only two environments: the antique shop and a funeral service. Had he not always been gray-headed and somber, even in his youth?

…This day, *today*, is the day I will unfold the tale of my time as Shedd Wilson, culture extraordinaire and family man, traveler and historian, successful businessman and fearless opportunist… Certainly the day was bright enough, even airy and auspicious when seen from the angle of a person with things to accomplish—perhaps more drowsy and cumbersome if its canvas was void of prospects. Nevertheless, our hero set about his task, collecting early journey entries and making chronological notes. It seemed to him that the accepted model of telling a tale in its natural sequence had been overwrought. If observed out of order, the events of his life, he reasoned, would take on a more miraculous quality for the very fact that the connections which made those events possible are thus severed in the eye of the reader. Suddenly, I am a schoolboy; suddenly, a shop owner; suddenly, a nobody on the football team—and again, suddenly, stuffing a pipe with tobacco on the white sands of Key West in black shorts that made my thighs hot. Oh, the dazzling silk of her legs that day at lunch, and—the phone was ringing. Some trifling insurance salesman. The familiar drivel about funds, savings, management, security. The hell with all of it, even if it was a sort of magic wand shedding dust on my poplars... Right, well, back to my Work! Where was I?

Newspaper clippings of bellowing Nixon, gray scale golf courses, a smiling belle selling her smile for Colgate. My potent coal-blue Oldsmobile, my woman on a spring afternoon crowned with the moist smell of dogwood and delirious wisteria; where the April morning was naked and dewy, the mid-afternoon is dressed in deliberate extravagance, primping and vain, longing for the moment when twilight unzips the gown. Oh, the brightness of her cheek, the clouds in her lashed eyes, the relish with which we ran errands hand in hand! Oh, tell me once more of your girlhood, the cherry pies your grandma cooked, the checkered shadows falling slantwise across your window—damn, the phone again!

Yes, yes...No, I haven't forgotten. Sure, it feels fine. Tomorrow, then? Yes, 8:30 is fine. Yeah, have a good one. The dentist receptionists always pounced on him when he least expected, as though they watched all of his actions in a glass ball and waited predatorily for that moment when there was a cavernous lull in his presence in the world as a social human. These moments gave him the sense that he was perpetually on a string, so that no matter how far he got in the world of thought and abstraction, he would be inevitably yanked back into the glare of polite 'intercourse' and practical matters. For whose entertainment on this playing field must I stay...?

Sinking back into recollection as one does into a familiar easy chair with a cold Arnold Palmer in hand, Shedd Wilson again ran his nostalgic eyes across the flickering screen of the early 80s, when on Saturday afternoons in October, Herschel Walker was scoring touchdowns just a couple of avenues over at the stadium, sending the university students and thus the entire town whirling past the stoic shop windows in a cyclone of Bulldog gaiety and nuclear-powered hormones, the smell of barbecued meat baiting one's stomach into a growl. Elaine, your Athenian grace perched like porcelain on a stool with Sumatran puppets suspended behind your head, putting more ice in the glass; I whispered to you about the rocks of Malta, the imprisonment of Cervantes, the fall of the Mongols; the twitch of her lips after she sighed, long fingers tracing the inner curve of a gruesome green gramophone, the form of which always suggested to me the frozen stream of a water-hose with one's finger on the mouth having flayed it in every direction. She said we inhabited our own king's chamber within our own pyramid which the great archaeologists had forgotten to excavate, leaving only us, paralyzed in the cast of this romance, safely outside the grasp of history. My father couldn't help but laugh when I joined the high school football team, puny and outlandish as I was. "Our business is the games of yore, son", and now of course, I know, I know...now, who could *that* be?

The doorbell was ringing. Shedd Wilson brushed the fogs of yesterday from his face and, with not well-concealed annoyance, made his way past the sun-checkered sofa to the front door. A poised young man with a gravely wholesome smile spread across his face, donning an impeccable striped polo and generally putting across the depressing sense of good breeding, stood before him.

"Good day Mr. Wilson—now, I don't mean to take up too much of your time"—Mr. Wilson's insides turned at this rank Southern nicety—"but I'd like to introduce you to the new Don Gold 4G internet service that's sweeping the nation. Our records show that you and Mrs...uh..." Here the young man paused precariously to shuffle through his sheaf of papers, apparently having misplaced the arabesque tablecloth meant to adorn the table he so terribly wanted to sell.

"Look, son, don't bother yourself," Mr. Wilson said briskly, "I don't have any sort of R2D2 internet service, and if I do, I'm sure it's working fine...!" The poor young man, so poised a moment ago, now openly gaped at Mr. Wilson with something between confusion and fascination. He almost said something, thought better of it, and turning on his heels wished Mr. Wilson "a fine afternoon". Mr. Wilson reentered the refuge of his home, muttering unprintable things as he tried to compose himself. How had he put it? *Culture extraordinaire...traveler and historian...fearless opportunist.* The words seemed foreign to him, as though he were trying to put on someone's ill-fitting uniform—too tight in key places, too big in others.

Mr. Wilson had met Elaine while dining on catfish and yams in Savannah, Georgia. "They *are* good here, aren't they?" she said in that irresistible, lilting Southern cadence. He had only nodded, immediately forgetting what the subject was. His heart became like butter in a pot of grits—she laughed in delight at the sincerity of Shedd Wilson's befuddlement. He suddenly wished he was wearing something besides the interminable flannel that, through a parade of shirts subtly different in shade and color, would sponsor the entire manifestation of his existence. Something more dashing, more hip, more…but it didn't matter—despite all his hang-ups, she was his. "Now Shedd," Elaine said in that way that always made him shiver, as though the very spirit of blue-crossed Georgia was addressing him, "Now Shedd, you need somebody to live in the past with, you know? Who are you going to talk to? Why, you'll perish in here from lack of good company! Look at that dust…!" And then she'd spring upon the portrait of Jefferson Davis or some industrial knick-knack in a thunderous fury of refurbishment. Suddenly the old Coca-Cola signs seemed redder, and the Charleston grandfather clock unworthy of such a hoary distinction.

The present was as inconceivable to Mr. Wilson as the future was to a normal person. Like a tunneling mole that has no use for the light of day on account of its blindness to it, he lived comfortably under the layers of centuries, ever burrowing through deeper soils. He routinely greeted the great Alexander as one is wont to do with a co-worker, even tipping his hat to Magellan when struck by a feisty mood. How Elaine made fun of me that one time in Key West when I quite naturally attempted to purchase a six-pack of beer with Confederate money! "I think we'll need more beer than that, honey!" she had chortled, gasping for air. My dear, you know me. Things only interest my soul if they are portals to another time—how can anything of today hold the same magic, the same chilling gravity? I am less an expert and more an addict—I suspect I've said it a thousand times. But that's still less than the amount of times I've beheld you again in my mind's eye, a velvet ghost in white gloves along a winding path, sailing beneath the moody maples, laughing in the shadows of the birches' white bark…You were never from today, either, but from a different time. My father said he didn't believe that I met you in Savannah, but that it was more likely I had conjured you in the dusty hours of an afternoon rumination. Take my hand, and tell me again…

"Hey, Shedd! Shedd! It's Jimmy from across the street—you alive? Listen, can I borrow your trimmer for the afternoon? Got some terrible weeds done cropped up again…" It was, true to the man's word, Jimmy from across the street. He had asked to "bar-a ya trimma" many times in the past, and Shedd Wilson normally didn't mind so much. Jimmy was an amiable, if oblivious, character in the neighborhood, the kind that is as native to Georgia as pecans and peaches.

"I 'as getting worried about you in there, Shedd. What you doing in there, anyway? Ain't good for a man to waste away inside on a day like today—make no sense, either!" Mr. Wilson nodded in polite agreement and led the vital Jimmy of the elements into his junky garage, much as he would navigate through his shop to find an old pocket watch for a wide-eyed customer.

"Man, I keep wondering what you gonna do with all this junk in here, Shedd! I told my wife, 'Hey Wendy, if we ever renew our vows I'm gonna find you a ring in ol' Shedd Wilson's garage!' Save us both a trip down to the damn jeweler's, anyhow!" Jimmy, as was normally the case, found his wisecracks intensely hilarious, shaking the eternal cobwebs with his belly laughter. Mr. Wilson handed Jimmy the trimmer—one that Elaine's sweet but ever-busy niece had gotten for him—and gave him a prim smile that was dug out of the Civil War era. (*Elaine, gardens bloom in enthusiasm for your joy, the fireflies are blinking—how the air in darkness glitters! My Cleopatra, my Athena…*)

"Now, you might say I'm crazy, but damn it Shedd if I don't like that pale look you got tonight, son! I—I, look…why don't you come over for a little while, have yourself some of Wendy's lemonade, and kick back a little? Won't hurt none…at least save me a guilty conscience!"

Mr. Wilson cursed his luck inwardly in various forms of rhetoric not familiar to the modern ear. His mind, in fact, was like a carbon copy of his antique shop. Various frightening forms of antiquity hung on its walls and peopled its corridors; doors opened with creaks, releasing foul odors whose source was undetermined; useless trinkets whose functions had been forgotten were nestled in a recurrent series of nooks; broken clocks croaked as if in protest against the continued abuse of linear time; and, in a departure from the real-life shop, Elaine's doe-eyed, white-faced portrait was repeated on the walls to infinity, and there, further, was a door opening to a pale Grecian balcony which, in turn, looked out to a wasteland filled with elaborate ruins stretching to a poorly-rendered horizon.

Quite defeated, with his autobiography but a twinkle in his eye, about as far from concreteness as our sun's twin star is from the solar system, our hero Mr. Wilson followed the implacable, fate-altering personality of Jimmy to his house across the street where Wendy's raspberry lemon-ade was entempled. He noticed how neat and well-groomed his neigh-bor's yard was, how much *attention* had been paid to details which his own eye would have passed right over. The weeds, moreover, weren't that "turr-ble" at all, were in fact quite respectable according to Mr. Wilson's judgment on such things. Here's a man, he said to himself, that actually remembers what happened in 1982, who in fact had things *happen* to him in 1982, or whenever. Indeed, looking back to his own past only revealed more things from the ancient past, so that an effect of concentric circles was produced, the outer rim being, say, that recalled moment in 1982, and the center being the object of his attention at that moment—something typically unbearable, like the irrigation systems of the Khmer dynasty. How onerous it all seems, as one inhales the smell of Jimmy's fresh-cut grass!

"Wendy, I told Shedd to come over for some of your lemonade—I went to get the trimmer but the man's in such a horrible state I had to bring 'em both back! Here, make yourself at home…Nah I ain't found that ring yet!"

He grinned at the morose Mr. Wilson. "See, I got her waiting for it now!" A noise of sharp protest came from the kitchen and Jimmy cowered in mock-fear, making eccentric expressions at his guest. Mr. Wilson, a bit deterred by the insistency of this Now-moment, curled his lips wanly and looked toward the kitchen doorway.

"Well, how you doing, Mr. Wilson? Are you feeling OK? Now, I got some raspberry lemonade that'll fix you right up—I know it's hot as the devil out there—and we can always call the doctor if you ain't feeling so good!" Wendy appraised Mr. Wilson's haunting appearance, a cloud of concern darkening her chipper face. "Boy, Jimmy, you ain't lying, now… Mr. Wilson you don't look so good!"

Shedd Wilson's attention, as ever, was abstracted—this time to a point just above the pleasant brick fireplace where a model ship was suddenly set into motion, a fine salty breeze in its sails as rippling waves tumbled into harbor. Ah, the spirit of the Phoenicians! the audacity of the rash Portuguese! Melville's brooding dark sea daring man to split its universe by mortal vessel; those seafaring Vikings boasting at nature in the incipience of exploration; only the moonlight and me in these lonely, rolling waters—yet it isn't the moon whose radiance tickles the foam of my ship's wake, but the true radiance of her laughing face, emblazoning the stars of my birth, for the ancients, as I, knew that the arrangement of the heavens is but a map of our inner soul, my inner soul, only her—only her on these lonely, rolling waters, and knowledge of naught else do I have in the cross-hairs of her brilliance—on yon salty waves, as in past halcyon days, I am found (Shedd!) and raised out of my cage (Shedd!) *Shedd!*

By the time a panicked Mr. and Mrs. Richmond of Goldsberry Lane in Athens, Georgia reached the faceless hospital surrounded by lilacs, it was simply too late. The doctors said that Mr. Shedd Wren Wilson, 62 years old, had expired from an apparent heart failure on the way to the hospital. Wendy Richmond kept trying to say something through her heaving sobs, and Jimmy Richmond, originally from Macon, stared open-mouthed to some point at the end of the hallway, his prolific tongue for once emptied of rhetoric.

Mr. Wilson's wife, Elaine Wilson, had died ten years earlier, and, according to the records, they were survived only by Mrs. Wilson's niece, one Audrey Birch who acted as a paralegal assistant out in Asheville, North

Carolina. She would see to the legal arrangements of Mr. Wilson's antique business and his estate. There the lone shop stood, an instant enigma, suddenly devoid of any reference point in the form of a human persona. The past, after so many years of resistance, had finally embraced her final relic. That its remains could not be interred there was the greatest tragedy. And the townspeople? They gingerly passed through its doors, suddenly absorbed into a chilling hall of diverse antiquity, of everything the living had long-since forgotten. The masks, iron instruments, puppets of the Orient—the eerie grandfather clocks that still struck midnight, like disciplined monks who could never die. It all seemed like an unofficial museum; in fact, it always had—only now its aloof guide had vanished. Many remembered his spritely wife, but somehow few of her details could be recalled.

The local newspaper writers gathered in their offices to write an obituary column. One Shedd Wren Wilson, 62, owner of Wilson Antiques on the corner of Oak and Carroll and lifetime resident of Athens, has passed away from a heart failure. And after that first sentence, they encountered steep difficulty in finding what else to say.

Follow The Scroll

An individual liker, singled out for your viewing pleasure. Unconscious of the eyes that watch his every move, he steps onto the travelator and propels through a swirling fog tinged with pretty colors—colors like pink, petunia yellow and aqua blue. His palms grip the smooth handrails and, chin up, he develops the impression that he is alone. Others have been here—*are here*—but they too are alone, anonymous and invisible as he. How perfect it all is, he thinks to himself, how thoughtfully arranged…

Sounds strobe through the peach-and-silver fog, mostly incoherent. They follow one another dutifully in sequence, but rarely have much in common. A constant fracturing of thought and sensation is the best way to say it. His mind quivers, shatters and recomposes itself in the scintilla of a second, which is ideal. The Likeable is best encountered off-balance, anyway. Hand on the surface of the rail, the man is casually propelled through a fog of his own desires, submitting fully to their unmitigated din.

The tipsy whine of a string orchestra slides into its typical flattery. Out of the varicolored cloud puffs a baseball rolls to the man's feet. Flawlessly white, its stitching is a dark crimson. *Sox need a new coach, maybe a liquor sponsor too. They'd play better under the influence, the slobs…*He's bending down to pick up the baseball when a voice interrupts him. "Whaddya think, skip," a voice says, "gettin' a little hot, dontcha think? Come have a cold one, I'll tell ya how I batted 400 in '41!"

Looking up, the man realizes it's Ted Williams. "Who'd ya expect, Joe Dimaggio?" With a chuckle he turns on his heels and, over his shoulder, shoots the man a follow-me glance. The string orchestra responds with a sly glissando and the travelator comes to a halt. A dirt road winds itself through the fog until the pair arrive at the weathered front of a saloon, which seems to lean over to one side. "I better leave the baseball bat at the door," Ted Williams says to the man with a wink, "only curve balls I'll see will be from the dames."

Neon font, sports memorabilia and close-ups of moonlit Jezebels crowd for space on the walls. The liker's eyes fall into a quicksand of arresting detail: the scene must have been witnessed *ad nauseum* by other likers, or else it wouldn't have been so easy to enter. Ted Williams leads him over to a semicircle booth with a chrysolite lamp hanging low over the table. Whipping his cap off with a grin, the Hall of Famer slides in next to a solitary Marilyn Monroe, who just a second ago was motionless with a pint-glass of ale held at a careless angle from her face. She tilts her head ever so slightly, and the strings melt into riptides of self-pity.

"Why, Ted, did you just come back from the diamond?" The famous cover girl is dressed to the nines, sporting a white lindy-hop number that bares her shoulders and coyly directs the eye to the precious point where burdened fabric parts. A pearl necklace drapes Marilyn's clavicle.

"Cryin' out loud Marilyn, my friend and I just sit down and you're already bothering me about diamonds—what gives?" Ted Williams looks at the liker and lets out a booming laugh that envelops the room like a cloud of smoke.

"But Ted, I—" She's about to protest in adorable, wide-eyed concern when a pale man in a beige trench coat holding a flashbulb camera slides in from the other side of the booth. His voice is edgy and grating to the ears, as though it were hailing down a cab on the street.

"Ms. Monroe, Ms. Monroe! Is it true that you broke up with Joe DiMaggio because of his plummeting batting average and subpar team morale? We all thought blondes preferred pinstripes?"

"I'll tell you what blondes prefer," Marilyn coos steamily, her chin pushed out and twinkling eyes half-veiled by heavy eyelids, "Blondes prefer Boston's Second Base Cold Brews, and fellas who are fast on their feet..." She holds a branded beer bottle up next to her face, staring wistfully into the liker's hungry eyes.

"That's right," Ted Williams says, putting an arm around Marilyn and smiling at the liker, "because if you've gotten to 1st base, you might as well steal 2nd, too!" The string orchestra reaches a glossy and satisfying climax, and the scene stops in its tracks.

The man lets out a low whistle and shakes his head. *How the hell they come up with that one?* He takes a heart-shaped coin from his pocket and tosses it in a metal chute coming out of the wall, just past the starlet's frozen face. A paper sign drops down on a chain from the saloon ceiling. The man rubs his neck, shrugs his shoulders and gives it a yank. The musty saloon promptly falls into pieces around his feet, and now he's back on the travelator moving at warp speed through the fuchsia-lipped fog, one hand gripping the smooth rail.

The conveyance is seamless and without delay. How can one describe the consciousness intervening between choice and its instant gratification? Not so much a thought or anything of substance, more a retiring hue native to the early morning, a mere transition between colors with names. Put another way, expectation living to be vanquished—an idea no less than holy to the whole operation. Unbothered, he gnaws at his fingernails, though the travelator in truth is more crowded than a subway train in Hong Kong.

Within milliseconds the liker has found himself within nose-length of a heavy wooden door. On it a tacky placard reads **ACME Green Solutions**. The door begins to creak open of its own accord and he steps into a quaint, low-lit shop which, given the abundance of content, seems to beg for more space. Slow Caribbean rhythms drift from the speakers and, between rows and shelves of transparent green jars, Bugs Bunny makes a sly expression as he leans on the counter.

"What'll it be, Doc? Lookin' to give the anarchy of your inner urges an external form again? Bein' chased endlessly by the rabid hounds of your restless mind?" Bugs gives a 'one-moment' sign with his finger and, turning around, begins to rummage noisily through a box, murmuring nasally to himself. He turns back around wearing a red, green and yellow bandana that ties his long ears down like dreadlocks behind his head.

"It's all in the uniform, Doc. Can you imagine if I was sittin' here in a black suit-and-tie get-up? Youda been out that door so fast I would've thought you was a hallucination from these here Orange County edibles. See, it's all about how ya present yourself, Doc. And I'm not talkin' that salesman psychology hogwash, either. You don't mind if I smoke, do ya pal?"

Without waiting for a reply, the talking rabbit nabs a set of rolling papers from underneath the counter and begins rifling through different jars, giving each one a deep, indulgent sniff. The big jars are graced with overly sensuous labels like 'Mango Wedding Cake' and 'Preacher's Mistress', reminding the liker of those arbitrary names given to racehorses at the Derby which he could never figure out. Bugs scoops a green nugget from the one labeled 'Da Duck's Revenge' ("That's a good one!") and begins his preparations.

"As I was sayin' Doc, a fella has to concede personal fashion in this business. This whole shop is just an idea. It's an idea in *your* head that doesn't exist separately from you. So if you're following me, alla your preconceived notions have to be wined and dined. I am Bugs Bunny, sure, sure...but who's to say I'm the Bugs Bunny you *think* I am?" He taps his head knowingly. "The idea's all that matters, Doc, never mind the whole cartoon shtick. All I'm sayin' to you is, things ain't always what they look to be."

Bugs Bunny curves the long ends of the paper upward and fills it with the pungent plant matter, which the liker can almost bring himself to the brink of smelling. The rascally creature hums a drowsy tune, as though forgetful of his company, and then with one skillful, fast-forwarded gesture completes his roll and pulls a lighter out of thin air.

"Say Doc," he says, sparking the joint and taking a deep pull, "you ever woken up from some dream, only to realize that ya still dreamin'? Maybe you was chasin' something you liked, like a big chocolate bar with legs runnin' faster than a gold medal sprinter, and just when your mouth's watering and ya think you got 'em, you wake up! You sit up in bed, scratch ya head, get up and go to the kitchen…"

Bugs launches into a fit of coughing, grimaces, and presses a nameless button to change the music (with a nasal sidebar). The shop's spacy soundscape is sacrificed for something resembling the Hungarian Dances by Brahms, with mischievous tip-toeing violins fit for an Elmer Fudd scene.

"Anyways pal, like I was sayin'…you're there in your little kitchen, cuttin' some bread and suckin' down orange juice. Everything normal and dandy. Then alla sudden your ex-sweetheart from 10 years ago walks in, you realize your underwear's on backwa'ds, and she's asking if you got the mail yet. Can you believe it? You never woke up in the first place, you're just in a different dream!

"Now whaddya thinka that, Doc? You woke up just the same dis mornin', didn't ya? What's to say you aren't still lyin' in bed right now, with your feet stickin' out from under the covers as your wife brews the coffee? And please, save me all the epistemological what-have-yous—it hurts my poor little rabbit brain. Da point is you have no idea what's real, what's not. All of us are walkin' around in dreamland acting like we got somewhere to be. Question is, Doc…how'd ya come up with all *this*"—Bugs holds both arms outward—"in the first place?"

The beloved cartoon's eyes are by this point severely reddened and reduced to heavy slits. A blue haze of smoke hovers around his head and begins to form a halo, to which he at first responds dreamily before suddenly grabbing a broom and brushing it away with mild irritation. Tossing his joint in the ash tray and scratching his bandanna-pinned left ear with an errant finger, Bugs Bunny allows himself a pause. He takes an old-fashioned wall phone off its receiver and begins to dial a number.

"Treedle-dee-dee—yeah, ACME Delivery? It's Bugs! Yeah. Listen, can you bring me a truckload-a some nice fresh baby carrots with a three-pound tub-a cilantro sauce? That's right. And I mean pronto, pal. Ya favorite bunny rabbit's starvin' ovah here! Say, Doc—"

Bugs, leaning against his elbow on the counter, continues to jabber into the receiver, but the liker can no longer hear the store's audio outside of the impish tip-toe of Brahms. A large voice booms: **"Just because it's legal doesn't mean it's any less loony! Come visit your local ACME Green Solutions today and peruse our selection of buds, oils, edibles, vaporizers, glass pipes and more—that's right, becoming a comic strip is just a short car ride away!"**

As in the old saloon, everything comes to a halt once the sales pitch exhausts itself. "Pretty trippy," the liker mutters. He fingers the heart-shaped coins in his pocket but this time refrains from tossing one down the chute. A simple draft of beer is more alluring to him than a smoke-tipped spliff, or any other marijuana mumbo-jumbo for that matter— Bugs Bunny be damned! The green jars recede into the distance as the travelator resumes its carnivalesque window-front survey, much to the liker's liking.

A miscellany of lights, sounds and movement are belched out of the swirling fog, as if the liker is floating in a spaceless pavilion of cherished noise. Images flash and repeat themselves; laughter bursts, trips over itself and starts again. The handrail remains shiny and smooth to the touch. As fast as the humming travelator races, it can only go as far as the liker's disposition takes it. He and the rest of the surging throngs of opinion-havers are, ultimately, prisoners to preference.

In this kind of interstate system, traffic is conducted in every direction at the speed of light. Each possible pathway is predetermined and lined with plotted pines and billboards. One only has to toss the currency of his emotions into a bucket to set the number codes of the central database into noiseless motion, that elegant cascade of data at the center of every liker's miracle. The chosen road is advanced, one could say, by the accumulated rubble of idle hearts.

Even so, the implicit eyes watching from the theater's upper wings are more the eyes of a single system than anything else; the event of liking is a flicker in its dark pupils, triggering a new set of outputs and yet another round of liking. Thus, it's as though our subject has just agreed to a contract with the dual scenery of amber hops and peeking cleavage for the foreseeable future. Such diversions— with their simple, uncomplicated appeal—make the life of a man pass with greater haste.

Our liker (for your viewing pleasure), perhaps out of a guilt-ridden sense of duty common to parents whose efforts in the affairs of their children can best be described as mediocre, now stops short at the entrance of a fog-wreathed building identifying itself as a school. To be exact, **The School of Emoting & Well-Being**. The liker finds himself standing halfway up a towering staircase which leads to an entrance flanked by stone pillars. *School of what? E-moting? E-mailing? Well, she does like computer games…*

The door opens and a middle-aged woman, dressed in a blue business suit, steps out and waves to the liker with an air of impatience. As he climbs the last stairs she somehow stretches her grin even wider. "So glad to see you, we've been expecting your arrival! Follow me…" They enter the building and begin walking down a long, empty hallway whose walls echo the rapid clicks of the woman's heels. Trailing obediently behind, the liker feels vaguely uncomfortable.

The woman takes a sharp left into a classroom labeled **Uplift & Enthuse**. The walls of the room are mostly bare, outside of a couple of stray caterpillar stickers taped at random here and there. Rows of students sit quietly in front of monitors, wide-eyed and still. What is most strange, however, are the identical metal bands with blinking lights enwrapping each of their heads like toy crowns. Learning appears to happen in a state of mild torpor. The talking head's monologue, meanwhile, is uber-rational—much like its manicured pixie cut.

"Here at the School of Emoting & Well-Being, we strongly believe that education must suit the emotional needs of the *individual*. In today's modern world, science is our biggest tool for connecting with the younger generations. These core philosophies have led us to re-imagining the way learning can happen which, in turn, has opened up new horizons of potential for our children…

"Every child is wired entirely differently. It's impossible for one-size-fits-all schooling to serve the needs of every individual! Actually, schooling *must* cater to the disposition of every brain present. We realized that in order to do this, our school had to penetrate the emotional headquarters, if you will, of every student's psyche…in the most efficient way possible, of course.

"Using new technology that reads brain waves and their emotional frequency, our educational team worked with scientists to create a wearable device that monitors the, shall we say, *algorithms* of each child's emotional center. The information is fed wirelessly into our computer system and helps us determine what sort of emotional programming the child needs.

"'Put your feeling caps on, I tell them! And—"

A separate, real voice begins to cut through the drone.

"Daddy, come on! We have to go. I don't want to be late for school like yesterday and Tuesday and Monday. Daddy!"

Outside of the imaginary travelator with its imaginary cartoons, saloons and institutions, Bailey sits at the kitchen table with her cheek resting dejectedly in an open palm. Her little leg twitches back and forth under the table. She isn't amused one bit with her father's intermittent grunts, groans and chuckles. Watching the seconds tick by on her watch, Bailey knows it's happening again.

"DADDY!"

The liker finally wrests his face away from the screen in his hand, as if he were a moth unable to resist the evening glow of a porch-lamp.

"Dammit Bailey! What did I tell you about raising your voice at your father? Huh? Can't you see I'm trying to take interest in your education here? There's all kinds of good schools I can get you into, probably better than that shit-hole you're in now…but all you want to do is nag and complain! Huh? Is that how you say thanks to your daddy?"

Her enraged resolve begins to fissure, and it's a great effort for little Bailey to fight back angry tears. She absolutely *loathes* her tendency to melt in front of her father. The 9-year old's bottom lip begins to quiver.

"No! You—you were watching Bugs Bunny and looking at weird ladies on there, I saw it! You're being mean and unfair, you always make me late for school because—because your face is always trapped in that *device*… My teacher says she doesn't like when I'm late. And I—I don't like it much, either!"

Now that his scrolling has been interrupted, there isn't much this individual liker can bring himself to like, either. The prospects of the morning's litany of demands barge their way into his mind, one by one, and his irritation is replaced with a great dullness which, ironically, isn't that dissimilar from what he enjoyed aboard the hazy travelator.

"Get in the car, young lady, and I want you to think about the way you're behaving this morning. Think hard! And you better not be bad-mouthing me to your teachers over there, you understand? I work too hard every week to get treated like some kind of criminal. What do they know about your true feelings and emotions at that school, anyway?"

Bailey furiously slides her backpack off the table and heads out to the car, slamming the door behind her. The liker looks at the black screen, inertly reflecting the sunlight streaming in from the window. He picks the thing up and turns to go. At least he can fire up the travelator just about anywhere, thank goodness. The things that happen before his next ride are largely insignificant and, indeed, more or less unlikeable.

A Search in Siam

Even after all this time, I can remember every detail of our introduction without fail...

He came to me between the layers of afternoon light that fell from the mountains across the city of Chiang Rai and its vendor-choked highways running north to the border, when the spiky palms are trimmed with gold around their razor edges and the rash humors of the markets can be sensed through every doorway of feeling possessed. The initial, blissful descent into the Asian Hades of night is lit by butchered cantaloupes that reveal lime-green flesh as thunder threatens deep from the sky's gray throat, is haunted by eels that flop in buckets like electricity caught in a bottle and the wrinkled faces of copper-skinned ladies who peer over them, is serenaded by a blind man who sits cross-legged on the ground singing melodies of Lanna glory with a child's keyboard on his knees. The dogs are languor-eyed in the alleys, the breeze brings a dense fog of basil fried rice sprinkled with red chilies that settles on your lungs like morning dew on a guava tree, and soon the evening slips away like a loose bracelet of prayer beads; the river is lit with reflections.

In this pregnant sliver of time he came to me, rather like a distinguished king striding onto a rusted playground, at least as I saw it.

He was tall, slender, broad-shouldered and narrow-hipped with a rich brow of kindness made handsome with concern. A wispy mustache lightly dusted his lips and the dark lashes leapt from his eyes, which as Solomon seemed to discern naturally the invisible forms of justice. His features were as pure as the morning rays that slant through the forest's canopy. He was entirely blue from head to toe, a solid kind of light charcoal blue, and yet his bearing was exaggerated all the more by gold rings that clung to his bare biceps and wrists and a gold crown on his head from which sprung somewhat absurdly a long appendage resembling a unicorn's horn. When I wasn't looking at him directly it seemed to glow in the corner of my eye. Thin plates of gold swam up his torso in fanciful designs, and yet one never got the idea that he was actually wearing any of these stupefying accessories; it seemed more as though they were a part of him. He had been scribbled by a divine crayon into reality.

Yes, it's true that he appeared 'out of the blue'. I was walking idly along the sidewalk with a satchel of English lessons against my leg, the afternoon imagery arousing in me a mounting fluffiness of being, when suddenly I heard a sharp crack and amid the barking of dogs, the screaming and hollering of the fruit merchants, and the clang of dropped pans there he was in his shimmering regalia, walking straight towards me, apparently unaware of the hell breaking loose around him. Some later would say that he initially appeared from around a corner in this moment, but honestly I don't remember there being a corner present to dramatize his entrance, he was just there. It's also untrue that he was carrying a flaming axe; this would only be seen fleetingly later. I remember a terrified German Shepard leaping over a 6-foot fence and the passersby who immediately dropped to the ground in vain attempts to kiss his feet, the women who stared noiselessly with hands covering their mouth and the screams that seemed to descend from the air like shining grenades, a poised monk who bowed deeply with hands forming the Wai in reverence and a tacky European who tried to get his whore escort to take his picture in front of the chaos.

He was like a residue of the midday's heat expressed in intelligent form; some held their hands in front of their faces for protection.

We departed from the market together with a breeze at our backs. I had many questions and he seemed personable enough. Still, he politely refrained from giving a name, as if only to heighten his enigma. The skin that shone like white-hot sapphire and the impressive ornaments that festooned it openly begged for him some sort of moniker, but ultimately it was of no importance. We were walking through narrow streets, haunted in twilight by a radiant scent of jasmine that seemed to emanate from the new coolness now surrounding the waning orange dome of light over the horizon. Mosquitos encircled my legs in silent festivity. He was an arahant sent from Mt. Meru who, as he informed me, under normal conditions occupied all directions of space and time in the universe and had some time ago, seven thousand years if I recall correctly, merged with Nirvana and reached the unacquirable station of being the quality of wetness in a crystal stream.

"In fact," he said, "I am presently speaking in Sanskrit as befits my person, but for your sake the words are *unveiled* in English, Mr. McCutcheon." I watched his dark eyes meet the sunset's light up ahead without permitting a glimmer in their inky depths, like a black lake whose surface remained blank of image beneath the sky's glare, and I felt the miraculous terror that we all secretly feel upon seeing a shooting star for having witnessed something so unknown, so vivid, so singular. "Why are you here?" To my astonishment, he replied that he had been sent, on orders from the alabaster throne of compassion, to the crown of Siam in order to locate the Lord Buddha's teachings!

"That's it?" I blurted. "Sir, His teachings are everywhere! There are majestic wats in each neighborhood, practically, and each one is inhabited by at least twenty monks. The people are giving alms, like, all the time…"

A Thai radio van crawled through the neighborhoods, showering its cloying tones over loudspeaker. His voice was as sapphire as his skin, smooth cool and clear, with occasional streams of light emerging from its transparent center. Thus he spoke:

"I came with the rainy season on a chariot to search for the nectar of Dharma, whose fruit is to have been sweetened and enriched by the ascent of previous generations dating back to the venerable King Asoka and his kingdom of sugar-lipped bodhisattvas who engraved starlit visions on the bedrock of their communities and sharpened their tongues on the grindstone of the Wheel of The Law, which as ever is turning, turning from Siddhartha's single sublime touch; I came, I say, on a chariot from Mt. Meru, and reaching earth I suddenly felt a great burden upon my shoulders like solid granite, the great burden of ignorance from the collective minds of all men, a sight untouched by the white lotus of Dharma, a hearing unscathed by the notes of His proclaimed freedom, for this immense void of lacking has its own gravity that even I am subject to."

He paused to adjust the plates on his chest, a faint smile dawning across his face.

"If I were to take these jabbering legions to my abode, an ivory fire would pass to their core until they liquefied, flowed through luminous gateways, vaporized, and joined endless waves of light in a shining hall of jewels, nay, they would know that interminable volcano that burps iridescent swells of color, and lucky are the ones in its molten path! And upon taking them back to earth, to their desires, to the pallid swamps of *paticcasamupadda,* they would falter in despair and stumble, for the mind that has absorbed the gleam of Rama's dreams suffers from something like sea-legs when back in the solid realm of Samsara. They cannot stand here anymore! This is the power of Dharma, and why I am sent to ensure that its mechanisms of morality still buzz along as intended in the heart of men's homes, villages, and cities.

"But we fear that, as the jagged cliffs on an ancient shoreline, the teaching has been warped and eroded by the long succession of egos and fragile intellects unable to contain the solar system of the Buddha's kindness in their scope, and so it is as we fear. You have mentioned the monks and their sacred order, the Sangha. We have created the Sangha to preserve the subtle currents contained in the Dharma, so that they are not totally lost to the minds of men. We have not, however, fashioned them in the manner of shamans or computer specialists, who do the knowing and perform Samadhi for everyone else. This fragrance was intended to be breathed in by the entire village, not just a select ring of gardeners! No, it cannot be said that the Dharma is intact, Mr. McCutcheon."

A breeze caressed the banana leaves and men stared from the belch of their red motorbikes. His words were radioactive against the threads of night spun throughout the air, above our heads, beneath our feet. Invisible webs of attraction entombed us all together, the smiling skeletons of someone's yesteryear. His skin had somehow become more sapphire in the growing shadows, and the unicorn horn appeared encased in the hilt of a fine glow. I felt unmistakably that reality was being flayed down to its naked center, but with each jab displaying more instead of less.

"Beneath the moon's midnight curtains I soared over fog-crowned peaks and rushing streams like a phantom, spanning countless provinces and taking in at a glance the religious experience in its present totality, its rituals and hierarchies, its peacocks and dragons and clouds of incense, its fluorescent pyramids of blinding tile, its hollow outwardness lacking the flesh of understanding. Everywhere I see the mortal image of the Buddha, but here his depiction strikes me more as a symbol of neglect and decay than enlightenment. Who in this land intends to enter the tabernacle of sadhana? To attain the lightness of the feather of a dove on the rainbowed winds of selflessness?

"Everywhere I have seen the likeness of the Buddha, as though I were trapped in a mad hall of mirrors that bounce the same image off of one another ceaselessly like tireless children at play; mind you, *that* is not eternity-it is madness! I have seen the Buddha carved in wood, imprinted in silk, paralyzed in ceramics and splashed on canvas in watercolor; I have seen Him sitting cross-legged in jade and emerald, in bronze spray paint surrounded by open-jawed serpents. But here his essence is as elusive as his image is ubiquitous. Nowhere does he exist, for the people keep his teachings chained to a fence just outside their hearts, which are burning instead with the snake-oil of the senses. If he has not a throne in every heart, his presence is enjoyed by no one."

The rows of spindling trees along the highway appeared to me as long fingers pointing towards the heavens. An odor of fresh pig manure flowed on a current over the solitary rice fields; dusk shuddered to its final stage of flirtatious melancholy. When his voice ceased in its discourse it was as though a light had been shut off, one that had been on for centuries. In the innocence of idle thought I had suspected that this life was some kind of automatic performance of blooming and withering, centered on desire, conforming to a hidden idiom of principle and yet still pervaded by what some call magic or the supersensory, others immortality. Now the truth confronted me like a snorting beast with nostrils a-flare, its horns aimed for the jugular of my soul. The mystery of his understanding had descended like a tempest, sounding its terrible majesty over the foul sparkle of the city where the statues of Mengrai stood wreathed in flowers and smoke, along the brown currents of the Mekong, through the quiet woodlands of running streams and crisscrossing bamboo limbs where neon lizards trickled down thick wet roots into the earth; a mute roar opened its wings and flew from Wat Rong Khun to the shaded palace of Kuan Yim; serpents decoratively coiled around heavy black urns stirred to life and slithered off into the brush; a lone melody shivered through the mauve-speckled trellises, finding the ear of old inarticulate drunks whose wives showered them with mockery in honor of ritual.

Intuitively convinced that he wasn't some sort of gypsy imposter or gifted showman, I invited him to take his rest for the night at my little bachelor's pad framed by *lom yai* and tamarind trees. To my surprise, he accepted thankfully—I promptly begged that he simply refer to me as Louie. Along the way his tone brightened and he opened up a thorough and somewhat obtuse discourse on the different species of flowers native to northern Thailand, pointing out subtle differences in the shapes of petals and explaining a lily's general rate of growth as related to the timing of preliminary budding. Through my confusion prevailed a sense of privilege. His terminology was that of a scientist yet his voice suggested a fountain of honey, glazing my senses with calmness and serenity.

He continued his humble elaborations on Thai flora throughout dinner, exploring chemical compositions, the practical utility of fragrance, the narcotic properties of the poppy plant, and even the rose's kindred insects in the most eloquent manner one can manage in discussing such minutiae normally relegated to the ivory towers of academia. He referred to lilies as "Mara's teardrops". As I considered the sapphire shine of his face it occurred to me that it wasn't outside the realm of possibility that perhaps he was himself a blue iris incarnated in human form, with the fragrance of its blossoms transformed into the sweetness of his voice. Caught in the web of his gossamer speech I remained immobile, savoring the taste of listening. Orpheus unfolded the arpeggios of his gracious harp before me, leaving trails of themselves in the air like amber echoes until my head was thick with the syrup of accumulated notes, and finally I plummeted into their gilded chambers with a delightful sense of perpetual imbalance, merging...

If now I am to become an unreliable narrator, it is only because the circumstances of the forces which I was subject to were equally unpredictable. Perhaps I am unreliable at reality's request. Was his appearance merely evidence that the cosmos has conspired to make a charlatan out of me? This would make your narrator, 'Mr. McCutcheon', the unfortunate victim of a kind of retrograding alchemy in which the progress of intellect is interrupted and reversed, eventually transformed into single-celled inertia by the influence of cognitions that are about as flexible as cold steel. Picture the catatonic schizophrenic, whose mania is expressed in aesthetic immobility—stubbornly frozen in an expired moment, unwilling to adapt to life's dynamic conditions. Well fine, so be it! If I am a charlatan, I am the happiest one alive. I cannot say how long I blindly bobbed on the surface of that sugarcoated deep; an eternity can be measured as a day, an hour, or three minutes. Who am I to say? What I know is that I woke to a cool mist brushing my face and a soaring silence that touched every corner of my being, a silence that instead of deferring, obscured, and even the act of opening my eyes echoed irreverently.

He was there. The sapphire man—he was out over my driveway about 15 feet away. Having taken my pair of white-checked black Nikes, he had stuck a sheaf of nag champa incense sticks beneath the tongues, lit them, and somehow levitated six feet above the smoking shoes in a cross-legged position like an African shaman in one of those dubious internet streams. Air Nike, indeed! A sourceless, crystal quiet was spread around a vision of cinematographic splendor, and even now I cannot say which preceded the other, but I know for certain that they were mutually dependent. For there in front of the gold-plated bodhisattva was a thick swirling sphere of gray fog at the center of which cascaded a magenta waterfall consisted not of water but of eight-pointed star-orchids, each one rotating counter-clockwise in rhythmic unison.

A dazzling dizzying dance of dissonance, had I the falling gardens of Babylon descried? Such was the sorcery that a single shaft of transparency fell diagonal across the flowerfall, just as a ray of light would normally. It sloped from the left downward; each petal passing through any of its points momentarily became clear. My senses were deliciously deranged, the normal power of sight translated into a peculiar dimension of tasting, of breathing, as though I had found a new life that could only be upheld by this soundless symphony, soul-sustaining, I slipped into the sapiential hypnosis of the wheeling, white-hearted starflowers in their soft fall. I have mentioned the mist wafting at a slow trot to meet my face with an old friend's caress... And seated in mid-air he was motionless, sapphire, motionless in the wake of his magenta deluge.

The routine mechanisms of spacetime had been defaced, thrown to the dogs, disposed of. I felt like a stranger to myself, like a lost soul in the madhouse of a bardo voided of normal human madness. His floral emanations teased my pupils, electrified me into forgetfulness. I was wayfaring outside of the mind's cozy constraints and—in that moment—no earthly Penelope could have cajoled me back to the Ithaca of self. The bright petals blurred in revolution and were splashed with inner patterns that arose, morphed and fell away, each one deriving meaning from its predecessor. The flowerfall exuded communication as its perfume. If I could report those expressions, showering in waves, my pen would surrender to a storm of rapture. Our language possesses no forms adequate to serve as a coherent vehicle for these aromatic cadences, hence my frustration...Faith itself is a language, but one cannot rely upon words to understand it. This is how poets are given the gift of sadness! Many times since that night I have dreamed myself to be a shifting pattern within the web of star-orchids, an essence of meaning only partially revealed, similar to how infinity is portrayed in every numerical value and yet is uniformly absent from all of them...

The next morning I awoke from a peaceful rest to the sound of chimes glittering on the surface of a cool breeze. It must have been mid-morning; the heat had begun to lightly flap its wings and soon would gain predatory momentum. I realized with a start that I didn't own any windchimes, and remembering the events of the previous night I bounded out of bed and through my front door. My eyes blinked in disbelief. Around a solitary dream-catcher of murmuring chimes my front porch had been transformed into a radiant pink altar. The same star-orchids now hung on white strings that draped the periphery of the porch and the sunlight was madly streaming through each triad. My home was in daylight decorated with the debris of his midnight visions...and now the bodhisattva himself was walking up to me in the full bloom of his routine beatitude, gold rings and crown reflecting the pink glare, perfect countenance a-shine. I wondered to what purpose that unicorn's horn was perched on his crown but didn't dare ask him. (Was it conducting geomantic energy?) He handed me a cup of ice coffee and a small papaya—"From the market"—and with a sheepish glance at his shimmering opus asked me what I thought of it. A bit taken off guard I stammered, "Yeah, I mean it's really uh...you know...really great. I think you have a gift..." Obviously, I had never made small talk with an angel before. He smiled a traffic-stopping smile and bade me come inside. I noticed with no small amusement that he was wearing my pair of Nikes, now taking them off before he entered the apartment.

"Mister Mc—ah, Louie! This morning I noticed that the walls of your bathroom have fallen into a mildly remarkable state of neglect. As a friend, I have resolved to amend the imperfections as a token of my gratitude." He turned his face to mine, a spark of mischief dashing across his eyes like moonlit stallions. "Of course, I am always open to reimbursement."

He laughed like someone reading satire but maintained the dignity of a poised Olympian. Caffeine allowed me to muster a buoyant giggle. It was more the sapphire man's personality than the market's ice coffee that was fast dispersing my morning fog. Besides, he rather looked like how I imagined a galactic lounge-singer in *Star Trek* would, a throwback to the days when the space age was depicted in gaudy Lo-fi. But not even the studios of Spock had ever seen such a costume! I followed him into my bathroom as though trailing the hem of a grandmaster's robe into an initiation chamber with, I imagined, maned lions yawning at the altar amid colonnades of candles... Instead, fresh-dipped paint rollers dripped on a mess of newspapers; crude fumes teased from my nose a sneeze. Half-christened brushes of different sizes stood propped against nauseating buckets of color. I wasn't sure what to say.

This magician, this guru, this astronaut-Gabriel...what had I, *Kru* Louie, done for him?

"Your stucco walls make for quite the task. The surface more resembles a shell-speckled ocean floor; rough, unlike the smoothness to which the painter's brush is more accustomed...Still in all, we're making progress. After all, why shouldn't a bathroom resemble a shrine?

"It is the innermost chamber of every gracious host's hospitality, the true measure of and final word on his character. The bathroom should, like the most glorious of gardens, draw yelps of praise and admiration from your guest. Indeed, it is not an equivocal point I am trying to make. When travelers enter a lodge of premium luxury, is not the first thing they gloat over and copiously post-and-share (I am familiar with you dear millennials) that heavenly lavatory with its reflective faucet? It is the prime symbol—"

An ironic grin had crept onto my face even as I tried my hardest to feign a maturity I didn't possess. He chuckled softly. "You must think I'm joking..." His right arm was in the throes of the classic painting rhythm: north, south, north, south, north, south, a dip in the bucket, north, south. A trickle of orange striped his blue chest and I thought of van Gogh. He hadn't paused, until now.

"Hold this, if you will, Louie." The sapphire man handed me the paint-heavy, sickle-shaped brush and stepped to the sink. I hadn't the slightest clue of how my credulity was about to be tested! He turned the knob of the right faucet, and where there should have been water there was instead a high-pitched, ear-splitting whistle that wreaked sudden havoc on my nervous system, causing me to send the brush flying through the air as I instinctively covered my ears and dropped to the floor with a nasty chill snaking up my spine. But the sapphire man appeared unfazed, bending closer over the faucet and making the hellish tone fluctuate as he toggled the knob. And then to my absolute wonder, the lush, hypnotic sound of a sitar came into focus, unfolding itself from the faucet and settling into a slow, liquidic flow! Such was my astonishment that I couldn't even articulate a familiar curse. His hand went to the left faucet and I automatically raised my hands back to my ears. The sapphire man turned his face to me and began to laugh from his chest.

"*Hen pi mai?*" He had asked me in Thai if I had seen a ghost. I answered back, "*Mai roo, kaap!*" And it was true: I really didn't know, but I must have looked like hell to him the way I was crouched up there against the wall with palms hovering around my temples and jaw open to full extension. Wasn't *he* a ghost? I mean, wasn't all this my imagination in the first place? "Don't look so out of sorts my friend! I apologize, fright was the last thing I intended. I can see you are a little sensitive. But take heart, this other faucet is only channeling the rhythm section!"

Sensitive. That's what he had said. Never mind that this blue angel-man had just summoned Ravi Shankar out of my bathroom sink, I was being sensitive! I was beginning to think of some methods I had learned to exit a lucid dream so as to be done with all this craziness but right then he turned the left knob, yes, and as though the knob were connected to my emotional state all of my petty anxiety was smoothed into contentment: the single sitar had now fallen into soothing synergy with the subtle verve of tabla drums, tinkling bells, and a quiet bass, and every now and then a snatch of human voices in conversation rose above the soft din and then (like dolphins) went back under just as quickly as though to maintain their saintliness by evading audibility. His eyes, darker than darkness, grew glassy for a strange moment and like parturient storm-clouds seemed almost pregnant with tears, but in an instant the shadow of that churning conceit had passed over and a flicker of humor returned to his face.

"My favorite radio station."

When I had flung the brush in thoughtless panic it had landed on the wall-side of the toilet where it was currently dripping forbidden orange all over the white tiles, and I now retrieved it for him. The sapphire man beamed at me and fell back into his work, noticeably cheered by the music. "My singing is never too well-received. I've been endowed with the ears but not the voice! In your society this is the only room a croaker like me would be tolerated to carry a tune, correct? Ah, well. I suppose if I *could* sing then perhaps I wouldn't appreciate the gift in others as much, and I would assuredly rue the day that my taste for any music ever subsided!"

"Well, you're certainly a wonderful painter," I ventured.

"It's the paint that makes the painter. The artist himself is brought to life by his medium. This was precisely the case with van Gogh, who was rightfully on your mind just a little while ago. Is there a better example in our history of a painter whose personality is so accurately defined by his style? Perhaps it is more precise to say that a painter proceeds from his own paintbrush. This is, at least, how it works in our imagination!"

"I never thought of it that way."

A pause. The faucet sitar rolling through the air, over the constant swish of the brush against stucco.

"I uh, I always liked the Impressionists, their use of color and every-thing. It's almost like everything's a dream with them, right? Or like how things really look in your memory when...when you only barely remember something, but the feelings of it are really special to you. I think that's pretty cool."

An encouraging sound issued from his throat, so I continued.

"I mean, that's what painting is about right? Artistic painting, I mean. It shouldn't just be, you know, the way stuff looks normally. I think that's boring. What's the art in that? No, I think the imagery should flirt with the impractical, I think it should represent the way we want to see things. Like a fantasy. Just like you were saying with van Gogh...I don't know how you knew I was thinking about him, but you're totally right! He created his own style of perception—the Realists don't do that. If van Gogh were to paint a picture of us right now, in this little bathroom, I would definitely hang that on my wall! Otherwise...I mean, you're really cool-looking and all, but it just wouldn't be as nice."

The sapphire man considered me with amusement. It made him handsome beyond words.

"Well now my friend, I can understand your meaning, and I certainly enjoy the way you articulate it. But considering the wonderful unlikelihood of this very scene, to which I'm sure you can attest, it would be a little hasty to dismiss the merits of a Realist approach to it. Take this bursting orange, for example. Have you ever looked at orange as it appears in the course of our history?"

"Uh, I don't...I-I don't think I get what you mean..."

"All colors have their virtues, and of course Truth is in the eye of the beholder, but one is hard-pressed to find one with more intensity, with more musicality, with a higher degree of cosmological fortitude and burning concreteness than the color orange, a perfect ray of energy. Let us travel across the human spectrum for a moment. In my Sanskrit, it is *naranga*. Once filtered through Persian, Arabic, and French it gained existence in English as 'orange', the only word lacking a true rhyming companion in the entire language. It has thus been the bane of verse poets' pens for centuries, the sole alphabetical unit that by its very constitution resists being a sonic plaything and instead requests the regal sobriety of prose. Is this a meaningless non sequitur, mere footnote fodder, or does it resonate that a color of orange's station *would* wreak havoc on a language that just recently has been foisted upon the entire world?

"Let us probe deeper. It is the color of fire, the primary element of heat, cessation, rebirth; of desire and attraction; of the ageless Dionysian principle by which planets are tuned with mirth; of autumn when the leaves lose their youthful green guise and grow old; of the glowing tiger as it explodes like a rocket from the brush. Its edible namesake is the pinnacle of all citrus fruits and yields the finest and most nutrient-rich juice.

It characterizes the delicious appeal of mangoes, carrots, sweet potatoes, pumpkins, paprika, and several species of Asian bananas, much to the delight of most!

"Orange is the color of the sun at its two horizontal extremes in the sky, and it can be said that the marigold exercises its charms with the same fainting fire. In Egypt, orange was the color chosen to depict the people's skin on pyramid walls; in China, the pigment often produced in pursuit of the alchemical Dream; in Europe, the House of Orange represented the very cream of aristocracy…

"Further, it inhabits the space between red and yellow on the color wheel and is thus the ultimate link between the happiness of peace and the hatred of war. In your culture it accented the unlikely triumph of the Miracle Mets in 1969, and it accents that same team's perennial controversy as well—"

"The Mets?!"

His face was woven with wry expressions.

"And speaking of sports, Mr. Louie, would your basketball game be the same if the ball was a punkish purple or moldy green? I am not here to say that it wouldn't, but perhaps some are sensitive to optic *malnourishment*. To speak more precisely, saffron is the selected octave of the Buddhist monks' robes because it is *orange* that represents the highest dimension of perfection and enlightenment. This is the same color that adorns the body of Krishna, personified flame of all creation."

Sapphire, saffron. Sapphire, saffron. "Is this sitar orange, too?"

"It depends…But let us return to the point, lest our florid rambling causes us to lose the scent of our subject! Orange has now been put on display in the full resplendence of its many dimensions, but perhaps you've forgotten something. Are all colors, despite their rich histories, not the illusions of man's mind? The visual senses, as you well know, arrange a grand mirage for the brain's audience. Thus, orange itself is nothing more than a manufactured novelty of dime-store theatre. To describe it is to grasp at a phantom's face...why do I say all this, you wonder?"

For a second he pretended I had the answer.

"The Realists recognized that life itself was *already* the work of an impressionism, an aesthetic signifying that disguises nothing as... something with intrinsic personality. To paint as you see was to capture naked deception in the act of projecting across the screen of your psyche, the flowering of mythical modes entering silently in single-file. Do you see? Life already *is* abstract! By its very root! A realist, then, is a man fascinated with quiet insanity. The impressionist only wishes to find a dream within a dream."

"So the Mets can't even say they have a real color...funny, though I'd still have to think any hope for a pennant on their part is a far greater illusion."

He had the kind of face that is nightly uplifted skyward, the kind of face that makes a child smile. I didn't know what was more remarkable: that I was talking baseball with a supernatural being or that I *still* didn't know the name of the likable character currently repainting my bathroom! It occurred to me that somehow the naked sound of the sitar represented the same message as the magenta star-orchids of the previous night. An excitable friend of mine had recently attempted an explanation of cymatics with amusing futility—I now found myself trying to recall what he said. Sound...visual imprints on matter...it was all rather fuzzy. Did the faucet sitar have a greater function than relaxation? Could it have created something that came before it? And what difference did it make that he spoke Sanskrit instead of English, anyway? I knew one thing—there was no local plumber equipped to fix this kind of faucet leak.

"This will need several coats," the angel muttered to himself as he bent down to swipe the brush through the bucket's well of holy orange.

"I'm sorry, but what—what is all this about? I can get my landlord's son to paint the wall for me you know, I can even do it myself! I really like having you here and all but... forgive my asking, but what is an enlightened being like yourself doing here in—in my bathroom?"

The jet black eyes sized me up, began to speak, and then interrupted themselves. The sitar music was the glimmer of light absent from the blackness, its notes broadcast from his pupils and running all through me like a hundred comets in the sky. He smiled.

"There is much to learn from paint, maybe more than meets the eye. I say this, you understand, as a prelude to what may be a long-winded answer. I hope you will not accuse me of pedantry here in your *hong nam*, though you must admit it's a bit unusual for a gentleman to be accused of such a thing here as opposed to the parlor or the porch where conversation is more natural. Be that as it may, I will start by saying that paint has two states of being: dryness and wetness. Elementary, of course! As to the causal relationship, however, it mightn't be what you expect. The dryness does not happen because of the wetness; indeed, it is the other way around. Wetness happens *because* of the dryness. How can this be so? Because in the wetness is the ultimate potential of dryness, the more finalized stage of being.

"Human life is the wetness of paint, Mr. Louie, a fleeting, flimsy thing that is gone in a second and *solidifies* into eternity. And yet notice, it is in perfect relation with its opposite state of dryness; what happens to the paint while wet is mirrored in its final state. The consequences of your actions here extend into worlds beyond the current one. To be more precise, the only reality of this life is its relation on the continuum to the egoless life beyond it. Think, could there be a world so transitory in disposition, so low of frequency without a changeless realm of high frequency to balance it out? Again, the paint's wetness arises by virtue of its chemical predilection towards a dry state... in the same way, you have been conceived for the purpose of attaining your final being, which has been in you all along. It is—this human life, this fragile being— already in harmonic union with the unimpeachable."

"What about being the wetness of water, is that the same?"

"To be the wetness in the crystal stream is to unfold into pure continuity. Present in every shred of being as an essential permeant, you are nonetheless absent from the tyranny of distinguishability. Consider the nature of reality from this angle! There is a formless light that form exudes and yet can't contain, much as language is a vehicle of emotion and yet inevitably falls short of expressing it. Form is the language you must penetrate if you are to find yourself on the *inside* of meaning. Words are just wet paint!

"It's a universe in which your own apparent existence is finite and flammable—so be detached, and be detached, and be detached. Have faith! Don't allow the mind to grow embittered with hopelessness; at all times you should be aware that your being is linked with an abiding meta-self not subject to decay, to the whims of this charismatic menagerie of sentience with all its *fatas morganas* draped over the horizon as seen through the eyes of an unreliable fisherman; no, with grace it occupies a summit whose air cannot be inhaled, where no stride can be struck and no word can reach. At what point is wetness dry? What did the Lord Buddha not say that he nevertheless wants you to know? Every moment is a brushstroke in which the painting becomes more fleshed out; *you* are the quiver of a drop. And yet you have already progressed beyond your nature, you are already there! The wetness of paint in waiting to become dry knows that it already IS so. Did the Buddha err when he proclaimed that Nirvana is now? There is far more to be found in what can't be said—Dharma sparkles in the quiet of the mind."

I inhaled his secrets with the orange fumes. The turning wheel had made me dizzy again. I considered the endless parade of things that walk, grunt, chirp, hoot, growl, whistle, scream, laugh, eat, lick, fly, feel, hump, dissemble, swim, shit, think, sing, drink, dream, salivate, die and live again. The dizziness of someone's forever…

"What is Nirvana like?"

His response was a shock. He looked at me for several seconds as though *he* was the one who had asked the question and only I had the answer, and then in silence he knelt down at my feet and begin to weep. His tears were streaming across my tile floor as the indiscernible human voices rose over the twinkling stream of the sitar. Thunderstruck, I melted, and soon mine joined his. Together we formed a bubbling Mekong River in miniature that forced my shower drain into a steady gurgle.

*   *   *

The bougainvilleas brightly swarm northern Thailand in May, as though the seasonal heat was so sensational in degree that it cracked open the living earth and made it bleed shades of purple, peach, pink, and rose like a terminal wound that won't cease or close. They border the highways like one long, quivering thread of reasonless merriment, individual thought-flares simmering in pastoral inferno, beads of dye dripping from the void in self-conscious rivulet—the accident of some watercolor goddess in her visionary effusion.

The recent events appeared to my mind as funny, unlikely outcomes whose melodrama was only afforded by that of my own wandering— outcomes not devoid of their own savvy humor. Thailand, I noticed, had a peculiar way of registering an individual's presence. In the case of some, this was exampled by treacherous episodes with ladyboys that ended in tears shed upon bed-sheets soaked in rice-whiskey. Others, compassionate gestures on the part of tuk-tuk drivers or somtam ladies which, bounding over cultural barriers like a loosed panther, were completely unsolicited. I even knew men who had killed themselves in this land of smiles. For me, little ol' Louie McCutcheon, the country was inspired into putting on the most fanciful of pageantries whose cosmogonic budget was evidently unlimited.

I was a young English teacher who approached the exigencies of his work with a steely nonchalance, resigned to his labors as long as the presence of his mind wasn't strictly required. I had grown accustomed to my role as the freakazoid *farang* in the eyes of the Thai, a foppish, minstrel-like character who attempted wisecracks in the local dialect and ate rice with the wrong utensil. I smugly deferred to this character and endeared myself as a puppet-personality that displaced my evolved American-ness for a rough-formed Thai-ness whose sensibility placed me at the level of an adolescent. Amid the bizarre glitz of this performance, my past became an abstraction and the future only a word indicating the next meal. My self was merely the bright rags of stage props and mannequin fabric— why should the resulting reality be anything less contrived?

As the sapphire man came and went, interweaving himself into the pattern of my routines, word began to quickly spread around Chiang Rai of his appearance. Because of the language barrier I was hopelessly out of the loop, left to make deductions from the frequency of visits my little place in the shade of *lom yai* trees was starting to receive. He counseled me to be vigilant, wryly suggesting that I start recommending my services for extra tutoring hours. For a while, he played the kind of game that made people who *had* seen him seem crazy, choosing to avoid public sightings through different varieties of misdirection. This made for some comical scenes in front of my house, expressive gestures consistently met with expressions of amused disbelief.

The supernatural emergence of the sapphire man was, however, irrepressible! One afternoon, as the sun roasted our soils of tropical torpor and admirable women dexterously plied their age-old trades in the shopfront shade, a boisterous group of schoolboys approached my property and broke into a distracting clamor. They would not be appeased by anything less than a direct audience with the rumored bodhisattva. The boys' faces began to take on a desperate fury that had a frightening affect upon my nerves. As their agitation escalated the sapphire man suddenly appeared, as he was wont to do, out of an unseen door; he approached in a steady gait, the crunch of tamarinds beneath his blue feet sounding through the hot air like an ode to his inevitability.

"It is well that you boys have shown up when you have," the bodhisattva said, addressing the boys in sublime northern Thai. "Our foreigner friend here—*Kru* Louie, na!– is expecting some company very soon. Your able limbs and timely arrival have won you the opportunity to take charge of the landscaping duties."

The boys gaped at this eloquent figure open-mouthed, intimidated at the prospect of responding. Finally, one of them snapped out of the paralysis and slapped the others on their shoulders reprimandingly. They all dropped to their knees as one with heads bowed. One head lost its cap.

"Come now, do not burden the earth with your groveling!" The sapphire man scooped up the cap with a twinkle in his eye. "Your politeness gives you the look of one whose shovel has already cracked the dirt."

The boys quickly got to their feet in a scrambling fashion, looking a little embarrassed. I caught one of them glancing quizzically at me out of the corner of his eye.

"Now, my wonderful young men, gather up ten of your friends in the neighborhood and return in an hour. There is much work to do!"

Expecting company? Why, I'm not expecting anyone! I turned to address my enlightened handyman, but he was already gone. Very soon, however, his preparations began to make a lot of sense. One bright day the floodgates opened, and my little lane became submerged in a sea of superstitious humanity; the people of Chiang Rai, shaken down to their atoms with religiosity, had deemed it fit to dress in high traditional style; such a regal, austerely apologetic mass certainly hadn't been seen since the esteemed courts of King Rama V! The colorful display of *kuam ben Thai,* of pure Thai-ness, betrayed the desire of a people in spiritual heat, prepared to mate with the Infinite. I was fascinated that they could all share the same heartbreaking shyness, as though each one was a street urchin stepping through a wealthy house for the first time, aware that any misstep might upset the celestial order in some incomprehensible way. I looked up at the sky; some raindrops that had rocketed out of the clouds suddenly reversed their descent and zoomed upwards. Their moisture permeated the breeze, mixing with the scent of jasmine in a way that impacted my senses like an asteroid of *sabai.*

They all inhaled sharply when he appeared. Gold plates gleamed in harmony with blue skin, and a unicorn horn pierced the air like a humming dagger of energy. It was his smile, however, that made them tremble. His voice rang out like a solar flare, engulfing the innocent locals in its brightness—their varying silk began to fluctuate in hue.

"If we are the body of the Dharma, let us be united in function! If we are to let the Buddha's name grace our tongue, let our ears first guide us to understanding! Do you think yourself incapable of intent study, of accurate mentation? Nay, you were *designed* for these very functions, just as the tiger is designed for catching swift prey! You are designed to *know*, even if that knowledge is so subtle as to be barely grasped. My friends, tune yourself with right thinking. Your life will mirror the rightness! You busy yourself with sand palaces in a windy desert. You are mature; why not busy yourself with that which will last beyond all laughter and lament?"

Cyclones of red orchids descended upon the historic, unsuspecting assembly. They outstretched their arms, radiating with infantile cheer, and formed big circles that slowly turned and turned, turning on the thickening carpet of red petals. Classical harps sounded through the lush air and I knew that Nature's operations stood suspended—otherworldly vapors were wafting over the boundaries. It occurred to me that my blue friend had made my home the new Eden; I suppose Eden was our home all along.

The descent that followed was, understandably, quite shocking. As the crowds became denser over the next week, more and more resembling a mighty river trying to squeeze between the banks of a modest brook, the luster of that first afternoon somehow became lost and the message of the laudable bodhisattva was cheapened. I'm not quite sure when it happened—perhaps when they hung garish Chinese lanterns from the telephone cables overhead which at night gave my little lane a fiendish gleam; or maybe it was when some sly onlookers scooped up the sapphire man's miracle orchid petals and started selling them down the road at the neighborhood temple, allegedly as a means to make merit. Suddenly the whole thing had taken on a carnival atmosphere, and it happened so quickly that I could barely detect the transition.

The sapphire man had made a habit of giving his talks to the community when the air was cool. Once in the early morning, once in the late afternoon. Local monks had provided a velvet, gold-legged altar for him to sit on, but he preferred to stay on his feet while speaking, arms always outstretched. (In the countless photographs taken of him in this pose, his image is almost invariably fuzzy and out of focus, leading some to question the veracity of this entire interval in Chiang Rai history!) The monks sat at his feet in a semicircle in their orange robes, reviving my bathroom conceptions of him as a personification of some van Gogh color scheme. The speeches he gave were never anything less than pillars of ageless wisdom, uncanny in their creative and illuminating interpretations of the Dharma, eloquent and almost playful in their delivery. I admired his grasp on modern science, and his insistence in emphasizing its importance within a universe that the Buddha had called an illusion. He even explained how the human anatomy interacted with the spheres through webs of invisible force.

But alas! As the days wore on, the sapphire man's expositions began to fall on deaf ears. Like uninterested students in my English classes, the people present struck a pose of polite attention with utterly blank faces. They were, amazingly, more captivated by the feverish hub of activity and consumption that this figure's presence had created. The margins of the highway just outside my little lane had been recreated in the image of a bacchanal. It can really be said that any Thai market is like a bacchanal, such is the customary abundance of pleasures, but it seemed to especially ring true in this moment when divinity had descended just down the street.

Endless stations of fried chicken, greasy pork, and yellow squid had cropped up; mounds of rice and vats of noodles sent their steam to the heavens; neon-colored, gelatinous sweets swam in sugar next to chocolate waffles; the ubiquitous *Chai yen* tea, syrupy and orange, streamed down throats for 20 baht and crunchy crickets were presented next to the popular ant egg delicacy; embroidered cloths, Indian silk, green tea ice cream; Buddha woodcuts and fruit shakes; bright, lewd t-shirts that said things like "Bitch Please" and often featured a Playboy bunny or obnoxiously-rendered marijuana leaf; vapors of vinegar and red chili encircled Hello Kitty merchandise while languorous policemen took in the scene with methamphetamines in their pockets; blind musicians played jittery tunes; teens flipped their thumbs idly across the screen of their smartphones. At night, lamps burnt in front of Ganesha portraits on the periphery, where the men drank their beer and ridiculed each other's fate.

The sapphire man seemed to take it all in stride, even while my vexation increased. But then one day even he couldn't resist the pull of full-fledged ire. A gang of well-groomed politicians arrived from Bangkok, claiming to represent some faction with vague allegiance to the prime minister. Daring to approach the bodhisattva at the center of the monk's semicircle before his afternoon talk was set to begin, they feigned reverence for his stature with an exaggerated gravity before launching into a well-prepared pitch couched in the royal Thai language, which they seemed to botch at key points. Referencing the fortuitous discovery of several white elephants during the current King's reign, they claimed that the sapphire man's appearance was equally, if not more, fortuitous, which made it incumbent upon him to accompany them back to Bangkok so that the nation could recognize the sanctity of the current political regime. Noticing the growing disapproval on his face, one of them attempted to placate him by offering to have a masseuse called in.

I saw it all as in a dream, one in which the emotions of the observer appear to be one with the events. Suddenly a pearl-handled axe was in the sapphire man's hands, and he was swinging for the fences. Not at the politicians— instead, at the air around us. Each swing opened up what appeared to be a gash out of which blinding light gushed. The scene in my little lane of *lom yai* trees was quickly obscured as the wounds in the cloth were deepened. The last thing I saw was his face, an island of symmetry in a chaos of molten flashing. I realized, right then, that this was what was supposed to happen all along. Now my identity was spinning faster and faster, seemingly around a specific point. It was so fast that my ego began to melt, parts of it flying off into the vacuum like cosmic debris. Each departure was marked by a billowing geometric surface of differing color. For example, my cynicism left me within the folds of a marigold trapezoid, my desires along the grooves of a purple hexagon. Body awareness had been the first to go; I expanded as a field across a body of light whose molecules were what earth scientists termed as "distant galaxies". Each form of life existed in harmony within my field, my corona-like projection.

And now with cleansing humor I remembered what was once "my saga", that of a little boy named Teacher Louie lost in Asia, stumbling through a smiling labyrinth of banal kindness, looking for a foreign boon, for the hidden treasures of the Buddha, for something I never had to leave home for in the first place.

Second Life of a Tyrant

The following is unevaluated information which nonetheless has been deemed worthy of further review by those possessing appropriate clearance etc. This letter was delivered to the Agency by a woman identifying herself as 'Eleanor' and subsequently passed to Mr. (redacted) on September 3, 1996, though the first pages are missing. No explanation was given, but it can be concluded that, given the volume of information the extant sheets offer, the missing papers were few and introductory in nature, probably consisting of certain intimacies common to separated couples. The following information is highly sensitive and thus inadmissible for public or private dissemination. Additional documents of relevance are included herewith.

* * *

…which I find myself becoming readily re-accustomed. Enjoying these Indochinese islands is a process of watching myself gradually vanish, until the 'I' recedes into an unrecognizable point on an archipelago-crowded horizon. Funny, that. If I allowed my normal mind to preside over the affair I would fret away my days in paradise, and be completely impotent socially. I'm afraid you know all too well, *min karlek*. So I let the neu-rosurgeon, the Doctor of so-and-so vanish in thin air just as the black fumes from scooters here in Langkawi…poof! It's almost as though the island won't accept you until it knows you're naked, somehow.

There is something addictive about tropical ennui. I can't quite figure it out. A fine line exists between serenity and excruciating boredom, between leisure and confusion. The Andaman Sea, as you remember, is meek to a fault; she brushes up against the white sands as if the island were a shelf of fine china. Not even a hard rain can ruffle her wavelets. Our European cit-ies occupy the other extreme, chaotic and demanding as they always are. We come here and hardly know what to do with ourselves. The Malays smile at me as they pull their boats to shore, shells shimmer through the clear, turquoise water, and I wonder what part of my life is really true.

You've realized by now, I'm sure, that I'm repeating parts of conversations we've had (in both English and Swedish). I'm guilty of being a bore in two languages, yes, but this is only partly intentional. The events of the past few days have left me unbalanced, disturbed, and I suppose writing these words to you gives me something solid to grasp onto. Thus I speak once more of the Muslim women, old and young, moseying across the sand in their full-length birkas at sunset…the quivering gashes of sienna across violet in the dimming ocean sky…and the speedboats whose long tails of wake-water scratch an aquatic surface of pure glass…

Still, I can only hide behind such exoticisms for so long before your eyes catch mine and coerce me into disclosure. It's absurd to find one's self com-ing undone in the shade of a palm tree. Perhaps it is something another cheap glass of rum can fix—you may rest assured that I've tested the theory exhaustively. Before I met the odd gentleman on Patai Cenang–by virtue of a mutual taste for grilled chicken kebab–I had lived through a week-and-a-half of the same listless day. The equatorial heat, if you recall, has a dulling kind of effect on the mind, like a strip of sandpaper slowly coaxing the top of a wood-panel into uniformity. Taken out of operating rooms, deprived of responsibility, I become an organic process of detach-ment, an observer without commitment. (I've had no more than one glass of rum, for none differed from the other.)

My nights were passed in a hammock facing the starlit whisper of the sea, reading Varela's *The Embodied Mind* by light of a tiki torch thrust into the sand. The light made strange rings on the white bark of the palms. Our English term 'reading' falls short in this case; it is better to say that the text and I found one another to be in resonance. Do you roll your eyes, my love? What I would give to see it! Still: a neural being reclining on a beach is not still, no more than we'd say a painter painting on a beach is still. The breeze, the bubbling foam, the swinging lanterns all originate *with the being*. A Malay fire-dancer would pass, flames tracing circles in the darkness, and I'd watch with a certain reverence as I looked up from the page.

Such moments were like the calm before a tropical storm. I felt this instinctively when the strange gentleman first turned to me in that fateful moment, the kebab smoke rolling off the grill up into the breezy Andaman air. It is the case after a week or so on the island that one begins to recognize every other expatriate, and realizing that you yourself are a 'known quantity', conversation (or the fragments thereof) becomes inevitable. I had seen him ambling up and down the beachfront sidewalks at mid-morning, a lonely figure with a certain resignation in the way he walked, which I explained to myself as the emotional mileage of a man who had seen over half a century of human folly. He carried himself with a desolate candor and looked up from time to time with the eyes of a hawk. There was a roughness to his shaven head and sharp mustache.

I hadn't savored the idea of a chance run-in, no—but I had the uneasy sense that it couldn't be avoided. We found ourselves standing there, finally, watching the stout Malayan woman turn long sticks of meat over a rabble of coals. He shot a couple sidelong glances at me and shuffled his sandaled feet. The moment seemed to bewilder him for reasons I couldn't understand. Clearing his throat, the gentleman made a vague gesture at the sea and, without looking at me, commented on the air currents. Not knowing what to say, I agreed with his assessments and said something trivial about the humidity. He grunted and threw up his palms up in a what-can-you-do expression. A little confused, I told him my name was Liam. "Salvatore," he said, grasping my hand. He guessed I was Scandinavian.

Salvatore was a brooding ex-sailor from Naples. He couldn't tolerate the idea of retiring anywhere else besides Malaysia or even, perhaps, Jakarta—he seemed unwilling to commit to absolutes, even as they rolled off his tongue, and often interrupted himself in seeming dismay. His face was leathery and browned from decades at sea; he was so gaunt that I was reminded of an expiring candlewick. There was, however, a sense of old-world charm and dignity in the way he expressed himself, and I found it easy to come under Salvatore's spell. By some tacit agreement we sat down on a nearby bench and ate our spiced kebabs together. I quickly realized I was sitting next to a startling autodidact and, as I am comfortable doing, mostly listened.

It's impossible to recall the entire contents of that first conversation, nor can I fathom the memory of a person who could. Salvatore appeared to have a fascination with the Stockholm school of economics, the details of which mercifully elude me. Quizzing my regional knowledge further, he managed to ask (after many self-negations) whether or not Pliny's accounts of mythical beasts haunting Scandinavia were in fact true. My rejoinder was that I was merely a neurologist. The old sailor painted Europe with an especially broad brush, condemning the majority of its peoples as 'degenerate'. He had a passion for Voltaire, and seemed pre-pared to defend him at any moment. Half-listening, I watched the dart-ing silhouettes of young boys play soccer in the sand, the sky ripening to a deep orange behind them.

His long-winded discussions began to tire me. I started plotting differ-ent excuses that could bring the conversation to an end, but the reality that 'pressing matters' don't exist on lonely Malaysian islands complicated things. Salvatore was on a high horse, galloping through the philosophi-cal wreckage of World War II at full speed. He cursed Mussolini, Franco, and the "willing idiots who every morning inhaled newspaper ink and grew murderous." The old sailor became more animated as the sun fell out of sight, though he hadn't a single drink since he had been with me. "The real blasphemy of it all," Salvatore declared finally with a finger in the air, "was that the greatest villain in history was allowed to slip away…"

This caught my attention. "You don't mean Herzog, surely?"

"The very same."

"The Leier of the Second Ryk, cult leader of the Neo-Boer nationalists? Come now, he killed himself in Bloemfontein at the end of the war..."

"Mischler Herzog, architect of the Broederbond war-machine, purifier of the Afrikaner race—the very same. The Soviets never identified his body, and so our History of the war's end rests on false testimony. Herzog lived, even as the Neo-Boer flags fell across South Africa, even as the world rejoiced."

"How could that be," I protested, "it's unthinkable! Herzog couldn't have escaped after the Allied occupation of South Africa, surely. And supposing he had, intelligence networks wouldn't have let him get far. I can't imagine it, Salvatore. How could you...?"

"I met him in 1956, on this very island. Eleven years after he committed suicide."

The shadow cast by these words is long and lurid; I shudder to imagine its darkness falling lengthwise across your morning walks, there along the swan-necked lakes where even now I see your face shine, noon rays descending through the pines...Of course, after he bade me good night I sat on the bench alone, stewing with scorn and resentment. Who was this crazy old man, anyhow? The rational mind goes to enormous lengths to defend its core assumptions. In a matter of minutes I had Salvatore pegged as a sea-addled miscreant, a drunken expat grown delusional in isolation, a sour curmudgeon filled with prejudice and probably bankrupt, too. The half-moon cast a long ribbon of lace from horizon to shore— I suddenly observed my tangle of thoughts in amazement. Had this stranger's idea of Herzog surviving driven me to so primal a dismay that I was willing to impugn the man's good nature rather than honestly consider his words? I marveled at the discomfort they gave me—perhaps you have gone through the same stages in the space of this paragraph.

No sooner have our doubts retreated, however, then do they return doubled in size with an even louder drum line. Why did it bother me so? Was it the thought that the most terrible atrocities in recent history had gone, somehow, unpunished? That their committer was allowed to steal out of some backdoor into an oasis of nonexistence? Or was it, rather, that History has so firmly reassured us that just the opposite happened? I found my head hitting the pillow at a nonsensical hour, somehow imagining that I was still sitting on the bench with Salvatore. Thinking myself to be fully awake, the situation went in circles, orbiting around the same two sentences in different combinations. *Met him in 1956…after he committed suicide…*Within the dream I realized the unreality of our ocean-side vigil, but more in a neuro-philosophical vein, not in a way that helped me see I was dreaming…

In the white glare of morning my anxieties appeared ridiculous. Young European children frolicked down on the beach and shoveled wet sand into little yellow buckets. Shirtless Malay fishermen pushed their worn skiffs into the shallows. I munched on buttered toast, washing it down with mango juice and coffee as my hammock lightly swung from side to side. The sun was high and the kite-surfers rippled across the water, their kites like painted fingernails up in the sky. More than anything I thought of you, of our time in Gothenburg haunting the canals of the old city and pinching each other's noses near the fish markets. Has it really been a whole year? It seemed like time had ceased elapsing—I find it bizarre to encounter such moments as the vapors of memory.

With a start, I remembered I had booked a tour of the mangrove swamps at eleven and hastened to reach the agency on time. I set out for the sidewalk, still shaking grains of sand from my slip-ons. The street cafes idly blared American pop songs that were popular ten years ago, as if the island was catastrophically stuck in an '80s time-warp. In my haste I almost tripped over a stray cat, drawing open laughter from a pair of locals smoking tobacco nearby. As I arrived at the agency I noticed that the sky had started to blacken, and the pretty Malaysian girl in the office told me, in decent English, that the tour had been rescheduled to a time later in the afternoon. A bearded Frenchman next to me struggled to understand the change in schedule and grew perplexed, tapping his finger on a crumpled receipt. The girl didn't hide her annoyance. "Yes…Rain! Rain! Just come back, 3:30…" He made an exclamation from the pit of his throat and, repeating the time, shot me a look and left muttering something colorful in French.

I looked at some photographs on the walls and stepped outside, pleasantly unburdened of my appointment. The Frenchman had already shrunk to a size no bigger than the space between the tips of my thumb and forefinger, scuttling up the boulevard between the trembling palm trees. How quickly the mood of the tropics can change! Only half an hour ago I was living in your typical postcard bleached in sunlight, and now dark, threatening clouds were rolling in from the north and the air was laden with the moisture of monsoon season. I could see a blue column of rain already shading one of the hump-shaped karsts of limestone in the distance; the color of the water had deepened to a rich emerald beneath the churning gray. Waiters and shopkeepers rushed to disassemble their umbrella-tables and lay down tarpaulin, yelling all the while. The sleepy street had come alive with anticipation.

Salvatore arrived with the storm, just beating the rainfall. He wore a light denim shirt with its top two buttons unfastened and a pair of brown shorts that left his spindly calves prone to the light of day. He nodded at me perfunctorily as if we had arranged a rendezvous, suggesting that we duck into one of the sidewalk eateries for cover. What especially struck me was that this second meeting had almost seemed implicit the night before, though neither of us had breathed a word of it. Just imagine, *min karlek!* In one sense I wasn't surprised, but I also couldn't help but wonder. The situation was sweeping me along in its own twisting current of logic, like those morning micro-dreams whose clarity increases with its chimeras. We waited as a motorbike sputtered past us, then crossed the street to a little shop with some empty tables inside. The sky rumbled and began to rip apart at the seams.

The two of us sat down at a little table and a smiling young man in a red apron gave us a pair of menus. Salvatore demanded two orders of *nasi lemak*, a rice dish with chicken smothered in hot sauce, along with a couple of beers, speaking in gruff Malay which the young man nevertheless seemed to understand. Right then, the clouds finally burst and the aluminum roof clattered above our heads so loudly that it filled our ears.

I fancied we were taking cover from an aerial assault. Leaning back and crossing one leg over the other, Salvatore looked out to the vacant street and narrowed his eyes like a hawk. We sat there like that for a while, neither of us venturing to speak. The wrinkles across Salvatore's swarthy face were like a map of his disagreements with the world.

The conversation I'm setting down for you here was one smuggled through the noise of rain, Salvatore's raspy words and pantomiming only possible between the imaginary four walls the Langkawi storm built around our table. In the beginning my cynicism manufactured a particular strain of pity for the man, but soon it gave way to a grim fascination and even, I must admit, a kind of horror. It fills me with uncertainty to put what I heard into print, but something in the dregs of this cheap rum, perhaps, makes me feel as though I haven't a choice. I believe it must be a similar feeling that compelled Salvatore to make this confession in the first place. For the sake of your patience, *min sota*, I've left out the unsightly tics within the gentleman's speech, such as his unsettling tendency to interrupt himself with "No, no, no!" before redirecting the course of his thoughts, or to answer in like manner to one of my questions—as though he were attempting to stem the tide of some unsightly fact while still upholding the appearances of conversation. At times his narrative became scattered. After a swig of beer and a sad look at the rain, Salvatore would venture into opinionated side-commentary of little importance, before finally re-circling back to the central drama. I have done my best to omit his worst excesses.

"It was a farce," Salvatore started, "that led me to the Jewel of Kedah in the first place, as this island has always been called. I was what some might dare to call a young man who in reality had yet to escape boyhood. I wouldn't have agreed at the time, of course. Too headstrong. As a little boy in Naples I had lost my father and my sister in the bombings, and so many others…so I took to the sea and never looked back. I left Naples when I was 15 and traveled up the coast north to La Spezia, where I found work in the Baglietto shipyards, building all the new race boats that would soon circle the world in the name of Italian naval prowess…

"In those days, the company was using its mass-production muscle built up in the war to produce luxury motoryachts; everyone in Europe suddenly had time on their hands, and all too many reasons to plunge themselves into the amnesia of a pastime. In my case, it wasn't that I had a great passion for seafaring—no, you see...I wanted to run from the spectacle of Italy at all costs. The Naples I had known would never be put back together again. And my countrymen? In the words of Voltaire, 'it is difficult to free fools from the chains they revere'. Beyond this, it is not worth talking about...

"As it happened, I was young, healthy, and hot-tempered: in '56 I was commissioned to sail—and I assure you I'm not lying—one of the first models of the *Elba*, two years before she was unveiled to the world. Of course, I thought I was the goddamn king of Liguria at the time, oh yes...the *Elba* was the first in a line of wood crafted yachts that would become the modern prize of *Nautica Italiana*. She was swift, beautiful, startling—a pearl in the open sea. And she was mine! The Baglietto executives sent me on her maiden voyage to Australia, where sugarcane investors with ties to Italian émigrés awaited their first peek in the North Queensland harbors.

"During those years I read whatever I could get my hands on, like a beggar scrambling for bread-crumbs. Headlines from the war were still branded in my memory. The Leier and his Second Ryk—ha! —had conquered my feverish imagination much as they had half of Europe in their campaign of Fascism. Sailing to Australia, I still kept newspaper clippings from the previous decade stuffed in my pocket...Mischler Herzog's malodorous charisma, the hell-raids in Johannesburg, the mechanical brutality of the Polisie, the takeover of Cecil Rhodes' diamond mines and the public execution of British diplomats, the Transvaal death-camps packed with Africans, expats, political dissidents—just like the British camps of the Boer Wars, only this time under the flag of Herzog's orange triskele.

(The human spirit, I was often heard to say, had been trice-killed in the span of four years, but this poor pun would only draw some snickering at best.)

"So, Dr. Liam, there I was. Even as my *Elba* parted the blue monad of the Indian Ocean, I was in fact imprisoned by my own...—what would you say?—...my own malcontent! Free as a drifting reed, but unable to rid myself of that most tyrannical captor, the past. I felt there was something more to my anxiety, too: a feeling that none of the mess had ever been resolved. In fact, many of us were aware that the Allied governments weren't so sure Herzog had died. Behind the raining of confetti after the capture of Bloemfontein, there were quiet doubts of the Leier's death, sometimes leaking out to the press and setting up the next day's refutations.

"I even remember...one panicky article in a British paper, assumptively a leak of intelligence, that presented six doctored photos of Herzog with differing facial hair—the idea being that the Leier could have conceived a number of (pitiable) disguises in his secret flight from Africa. What amused me most, doctor, was that not one of them appeared to succeed in concealing who he was—the beard of a rabbi seemed to do little better than his customary thin-cut mustache in deflecting attention, such was the unmistakable look in those beady, withering eyes...To be sure, the evidence for suicide was scant—it relied upon questionable eyewitnesses to reach a sweeping conclusion.

"Most of what the common man knows is apocryphal, do you agree? He is impressionable, neurotic, easily persuaded, and wars only increase these conditions threefold. The common man was too satisfied with the story's end to be scientific about Herzog's fate. Our high seas, however, were crisscrossed with lines of espionage, and we'd heard enough in our voyages to suspect that the warlord hadn't reached such a tidy end, after all. Some accounts placed him in bizarre locales—rural France, Detroit, Michigan—which I chalked up to hysteria. Most accounts, however, had Mischler Herzog escaping ...via an underground tunnel and being flown to the coast by a Neo-Boer pilot, whence he was conducted to Borneo via Japanese submarines.

"After nearly two months at sea, we arrived in North Queensland without incident and at once availed ourselves of a local brothel, where I was surprised to meet, eventually, the sugar businessmen who had failed to meet us in the harbor several days before. They were of the colonial stock and strutted in and out of saloons with great pomp, making claims of 'attending to business' but never once permitting me to pursue the topic of my appointment. These high-society men, I realized, drowning in the spoils of their sugar profits, had grown dull-witted in complacency. For an entire week I was rarely sober by noon—no, no, no…it was only in slumber that I was sober at all! Meanwhile my comrades had abandoned me, likely to find work at a mill friendly to Italians…

"It was only when I threatened to leave that the louses, with much shoulder-slapping and putting on of airs, agreed to come down to the docks for a look at my *Elba*. I found her idle and reclined against the dock, long wooden hull shaded rosy in the gloaming…I was ashamed, you see, to bring her into the company of such drunken idiocy. *Così è la vita!* I had no choice in the matter. Once the businessmen had made a show of inspecting her (though it was clear their familiarity with a good boat's anatomy didn't exceed their understanding of politics), they somberly turned to me with a request: They asked that I demonstrate the *Elba*'s worthiness by taking a group of Australian geologists to the region of Malaya, where they wished to do a formal survey of some sort–Ha! It wasn't too far, they said, and after ten days we'd make our return to North Queensland. I was enraged, but helpless. The Baglietto big-wigs would jump at the chance to boast of their new yacht rippling through Asian waters. I looked at the moon, spat in the water and nodded my head. Within two days, we were off…

"It never occurred to me, Dr. Liam, that we were headed straight for the epicenter of Herzog's legend until—no, no—until a day or two after we'd rounded the northern coast of Papua New Guinea, following the currents that would eventually lead us through the gates of Indonesia into the Strait of Malacca. I admit that—yes—for a moment I was seized with foreboding; I clutched at the clippings in my pocket, tore one into pieces and flung it overboard, as though I'd been made the butt of a joke. The next moment I let out a great laugh—the sea was talking me into delirium. Who was such a man to me, anyhow? Nothing more than *idea*, shapeless, devoid of flesh and blood! The four geologists had themselves sufficiently unnerved me, circumspect and secretive as they were. Those men didn't have conversations so much as they muttered to themselves in the company of one another…

"But my treasured *Elba*, in spite of our odd passengers (or, perhaps, because of them), approached the foot of Malaya with great dispatch, shooting the long corridor of Malacca unscathed by its pirates, who, you may have heard, make a living from hijacking the big freighters to and from Singapore. The rock-lovers had decided to forego Borneo for the obscure islands of Langkawi; we shot up the western coast of Malaya, drifting past Penang, then Sumatra, lurching through the terrible Andaman depths under black, star-torched skies. And then, finally, the region of Kedah just south of the Thai border—I kicked the old girl up to 20 knots until the mammoth sea-stacks began to appear on the horizon, like monuments built by a race of Giants (despite my many vices, doctor, I am even now a skilled navigator)…

"Only later did I learn of the island's curse—which, centuries ago, sprang from the lips of a maiden awaiting execution on account of another woman's jealousy—and yet even while we approached the southern shore I fancied that we'd crossed into a forbidden place. The air was perfectly still, windless, as if the ghost of Mahsuri held her breath—sunset rendered the sky a burning ember bruised purple and red, spreading like wildfire through the surrounding infinity of water…Silently we passed between hoary sea-stacks that seemed to vault the very clouds themselves, their crowns circled by seagulls. A school of dolphins trailed us on the starboard side like dutiful escorts of Fate. Even when the four geologists started their inevitable jabbering I remained aghast in enchantment, for I could see her lips were sealed…ah, Dr. Liam…!

"Forgive this bitter old man's digressions: of course, our company numbered greater than dolphins—it wasn't long before we saw the islanders' fishing boats gliding through the dusk, their mast-head lamps letting off a dim glow between the depths of sky and sea, and a glance ashore afforded us a view of the villagers' *kampong* flickering with torch-lights along the narrow strip of sand, where the fishermen kept all manners of junks, rigs, vessels and sampans moored in the shallows. The smell of burning driftwood reached our nostrils and Malayan voices called out to us in greeting; it wasn't a civilization I recognized, no…but *civilization* nonetheless!

"The reception caught me by surprise. We were met by a beaming committee of shirtless men, old and young, who made great haste in pulling us to shore and helping us disembark; this was owing to the fact that my grave companions of science had a contact on the island, another poor fellow laboring under the auspices of the Geological Society in Langkawi's interior, who was evidently fluent in the local dialect. The natives, meanwhile, openly marveled at my *Elba*, gushing over her angled beauty in a tongue I would only come to understand after decades. I watched as their teeth shone in the dancing shadows.

"Gradually, by means of exaggerated gestures, our party was escorted to a towering bonfire situated in a ring of tall, bending cocoa palms, beyond which I could make out some bamboo huts raised off the ground on wooden stakes. We were treated to smoked fish, devouring the flesh ravenously as the young women pretended not to stare. A young man came forward, then, introducing himself as Sullah in faltering English. A gilded tiger-claw hung from his neck and he bore a long scar across his cheek, but his mannerisms I found most agreeable. Sullah informed us of the arrangements: the four geologists were to report to Dr. Laramie first thing in the morning—as for me, I was at liberty to remain with the villagers…a prospect which, as you may have guessed, didn't upset me in the least.

"Sullah led me to an empty bamboo hut nestled in a grove of mangosteen trees, where the night was so inky black that I needed his help climbing up the ladder to get in. He struck a match and lit three candles, illuminating a small room of dirt floor covered with woven sleeping mats richly striped in heliotrope and light chartreuse green, threaded gold across the borders. (The designs are still distinct in my memory…) Sullah considered my presence for a moment with some curiosity, then kneeled down next to me. There was an middle-aged white man, he told me, whom I would see there in the rice paddy fields in the morning. He spoke little English, and of him the Malays knew almost nothing. I felt my insides, doctor, go very cold. Perhaps he was a *pa-wang*, Sullah opined—a wizard of some sort. I only nodded my head, and soon Sullah took his leave.

"The night's stillness was fringed by the gentle lapping of the tide. I found myself half-submerged in sleep, my crowding thoughts converted into the bustling rhythms of a town-square. The mind watched itself resist what was already self-evident: the Leier hadn't perished, he'd only disappeared. Now I, too, was out of Europe's sight—we were to meet under the presumption of impossibility. Legends of the war once again flashed before me...the black tunic of the S.A.P., a triskele sharply emblazoned on the armband; the Broederbond summoning spirits of Celtic potentates as they burned effigies of Zulu warriors in the glee of ritual; the conquest of Africa, extermination of her peoples and appropriation of her relics in the name of the Second Ryk, measuring its progress in munitions and bloodshed. You shake your head, Dr. Liam, and so do I. The Neo-Boers lapsed into a piety for the occult, then a whole nation unknowingly followed suit. As for me, the night was humid, and I found myself badly in need of a mosquito net.

"The morning finally greeted our little island, and Sullah led me to the rice paddies after a breakfast of coconuts in the warm sand, served by a little monkey the islanders call a *brok*. (Have you seen them?) To get there, we had to follow a trail beaten through a dense, steamy swathe of jungle: a culmination of tangled undergrowth and long, looping vines unlike anything I'd ever seen. A variety of noises rained down upon us from the inner folds of the canopy, as though from another world invisible to foreign eyes. My paranoia was only relieved by Sullah—with alacrity he assured me he'd already made peace with the jungle spirits.

"I was given no reason to doubt him, as soon we exited the maze of vegetation and came upon the busy rice paddies. It was towards the end of the year—harvest season—and the stalks of rice stood tall and golden across an endless field, unveiled by a white mist slowly lifting up into the morning brilliance. The men trudged behind their buffalo-drawn carts, shielding their eyes from the sun, while the women winnowed the fine grain in festive *sarongs*. It didn't take long to see him, even before Sullah directed my attention to his figure. A nuclear chill ran through my bones. There stood the once-terrible dictator, muddied trousers rolled up to his knees in the shallow water, painfully swinging a rusty *tajak* through a patch of rice.

"There, doctor, was a specter capable of bringing society to its knees. As it was, merely one mind was present to absorb the shockwaves. I began to walk toward Herzog, at first unsteadily and then with greater purpose. I can read the question in your eyes—yes, for a moment I considered plunging Sullah's sharpened *kris* into his unsuspecting gut...but instead something resembling pity took over me. His face was consumed in a mess of stubble that spread down his neck, and his menacing coiffure had long-since submitted to balding. As I drew nearer I could see his skin had grown pale and almost yellow, like a consumptive. (Genocide, perhaps, hadn't been easy on his liver...) The Leier received my approach with a chilly stare.

"Beyond the terrifying shock of recognition, I couldn't understand the vision before me. What authority could sentence Mischler Herzog to manual labor among a group of villagers, besides that of his own conscience? He stiffly leaned against his instrument and took stock of me, seemingly void of malice. Despite the dictator's miserable appearance, I noticed that his clothing was generally clean and well-fitted. It was clear that his needs were taken care of; I could only guess that he was here of his own volition. Bewildered, I nodded my head. He mumbled something I couldn't understand and began walking to a group of palm trees at the edge of the fields. An older woman offered Herzog some morsel as he passed, which he took with satisfaction. The villagers tittered cautiously—they were circumspect in their dealings with the strange man, for they could innately sense he was capable of vast cruelties.

"And yet, doctor, there was something so humbled, so *altered* in his manner, as if he had denounced his own historical figure in order to salvage the last bit of humanity available to him—how can I explain it? The pagan castles of the Transvaal having evaporated, the Second Ryk now toppled upon its own foundations, Herzog had resigned himself to the simplicity of a rural life lived out in secret—his own life after death. I sat next to him on the ground beneath the swaying palms, watching the harvest as I chewed on a square of rice. He made some funny noises in his throat, and after a while started to speak in a commanding strain of Afrikaans. I listened in silence. It was doubtful any of the Leier's comments were addressed to me.

"After a couple of minutes, an orange-breasted kingfisher alighted near our spot in the shade. He sank his long bill into the ground, allowing the Malay sunlight to coruscate across his indigo crown. Herzog grew excited, apparently losing track of his dense musings. *"Vlinder,"* he repeated, *"Vlinder!"* We watched the fanciful thing until it abandoned its search and flew out of sight. Not until years later did I learn that Herzog was comparing the kingfisher to a butterfly in his native tongue, but in the moment my intuition served...I started to tremble mightily, for the greatest abomination of all had started to occur within my chest. I felt myself warming to this pitiful, lonesome man...I felt myself, against all ethical and spiritual instincts, sympathize with Mischler Herzog, the maniacal tyrant..."

Salvatore broke off abruptly, his voice unable to remain steady. I cleared my throat, trying to collect myself. The downpour had finally ceased— fragile beams of light found their way through parting clouds into rean- imated streets, where the island's playfulness once again peeked its head out from opened shutters. I remember thinking I had never breathed air so clear as in that passing instant. Salvatore stood up then, and with an air of confession, lifted a corner of his shirt: against the bare flesh of his ribs was a black triskelion in its silent whirl, and the old man turned his face away in shame.

[STAMPED]

The Scorekeeper

Chapter One

"*A*nd one!" a blue-booted, airborne blur screams. The orange sphere hangs in the air, a grapefruit at the tip of an invisible branch, then kisses the rickety ring twice before falling through a gray net.

"And one, nothing!" The aggressor's lips spread into a smile of amused disgust as he surveys his grounded opponent. "You see any TV cameras out here? No one's playing that touch-foul nonsense!"

A forest of heads assembles beneath the hoop. The forest's breath is white in the cold air.

"You know what," announces the headbanded figure, "little guy's trying to get them Kobe calls…must be all them sorority girls he's talking to!"

The scorer, glaring up at the jeering giant from the mottled cement, now folds knees to chest and bolts upward. "That's funny," he ventures, his lashed eyes defiant amid the laughter, "because I know you haven't gotten anything since *Nash* was the MVP…!"

The forest is hit by a hurricane and bodies furiously join, blend, thrash and separate. The ball rolls quietly to the sideline like errant litter, for the moment excluded from its own drama.

"Hey, hot-blooded dummies," a deep-throated, raspy voice suddenly rises into the chilly air, "the less ball you playin', the more I start thinking about what's for dinner!" Heads turn. A slow wave of resignation halts the baleful tango.

"Now are y'all gonna finish this game, or what?"

The forest bows and disperses into individuals. One is still struggling: the big python-armed aggressor in the red headband. "Come on Bank, let's just finish this game and be out, man! We didn't pay that old man to watch us brawl. Hey— " Bank-Shot Davis tries to wrest the fists from his jersey's powder-blue numbers. "Hey, look! We're gonna whip these suckers anyway. Don't worry about that fool…"

Bank looks at the old man leering from the bleachers, a young boy in glasses next to him. The day's dark clouds are becoming the evening's total darkness.

"Alright man, I'm good! But if that uppity punk says something else…" On the other side of the court, the subject makes a dismissive gesture at the pair with his right hand. The sharp red of his team uniform against the court's desolate gray gives a sense of unauthorized color. Besides some drifters behind the bleachers, the neighborhood's bare beech and box-elder trees claim exclusive attendance.

"One free throw, Jedi Jamal," the old man rasps, squinting at the paper in his hands. The two teams congeal at the far end, arranging themselves in the proper positions like self-directed chess pieces. Jamal is at the free-throw line.

One dribble, a second, a third…his high-arcing shot is true. "Tie game at 45, first to 50, boys…" The action charges in the other direction. "Five for five now, isn't he?" The young boy, Tiresias, consults a scrawled grid of squiggly numbers and slanted tallies, pushing his glasses up the bridge of his nose. "Six for six, sir."

The old scorekeeper nods absentmindedly, his foggy pupils following the ball's trip around the perimeter. Like a comet, it zips astrally from one set of hands to another until it reaches Bank down on the block; he backs down his man with a dribble, feigning a post attack, and then whips it right back out to the corner for an open three…

…the lanky shooter cans it, unlocking a primal yell from deep within the bulk of Bank.

The grizzled face shakes its head. "48 to 45, baby blue…" A February draft momentarily kidnaps the March twilight; the power lines tremble along their sinuous geometries. "Time was," the scorekeeper mutters to himself, "a fella couldn't wear the other team's colors without being sent back to his house with the quickness."

The park's lights flicker on with a faint buzz.

The names may change, but the players never do.

Young, clean-shaven Jamal morphs into a flamboyantly bearded Walt Frazier and, jumping a high screen, splits the defenders, pirouettes around another at the elbow…

Ol' Frazier, boy!

…gathers himself and takes flight, but is met squarely in the air by a multi-armed wall—crafty Frazier slithers his left arm around his defender's hip and the ball pops into a teammate under the rim.

Anointed king of New York in 1970; his Knicks were the toast of the town.

The red team has pulled to within one. "That Jamal," the little voice to the scorekeeper's side pipes up, "sure can play can't he, grandpop?" The old man affirms with a curt nod. "Sure can, son…"

Red jerseys sway like cobras as baby blue advances the ball across half-court. An angry honk sounds twice from up the street but no one seems to hear. Bank sets a pick for his point guard above the three-point arc and immediately senses empty space in front of him. "RONNIE!" he bellows, arms in the sky.

The desolate cement is now a glossy hardwood, the vacant bleachers a multi-tiered interior of an arena peopled by tens of thousands.

Here in DC, we had big ol' Elvin Hayes at power forward…

Bank swipes Ronnie's pass out of the air with the classic stripes of the Washington Bullets emblazoned across his chest. A pump-fake sends one defender into the air; his face stares downward helplessly.

Run for cover when Big E gets a-rumbling!

The barrel-chested forward now puts his head down and bullies into the paint, red headband pulsating like an evolutionary warning signal. The crowd holds its breath in anticipation.

Elvin, for the win…

"Shit!" His contested layup ricochets too hard for the rim to catch—the red team gathers the rebound. The packed stands fade away and the garish logo at center court is swallowed back up by the dullness of concrete.

Jamal receives the outlet pass in stride but elects to slow the pace. Bodies are flashing past in the animation of their uniform colors. Dribbling contemplatively from the right sideline to center court, only Jamal's face remains distinct.

The right play has already started to happen, all you have to do is stay with the rhythm.

The swingman emerges from the squirming jungle of the paint and rockets out to the left wing.

"Stay up! Stay up!"

Jamal rifles it to him. The player's intention to shoot is clear, but the way is not; a series of pivots and up-fakes does little to upset the defender's focus. The long-armed guard puts the ball on the ground and drives right, but is cut off by Elijah's sagging defender.

"Get back! Get back!"

The ballhandler, however, has already sensed the fatal mistake. He picks up his dribble and, lifting himself slightly into the air, flips the ball over the defender's head back to Jamal.

When guys are coordinated, it's like one motion...

The point guard has just enough daylight to get the three-pointer off–his release is swift. Bags of popcorn drop from the fingers of gaping, ghostly onlookers. His shooting hand has settled into an ominous goose-neck.

Shoop. So pure, the net could have kept it a secret from the rim.

"Game, red team!" The victors bump fists in weary acknowledgement. "Come pay for your stats or I throw 'em to the rats..." Bank's face is scrunched up as though registering a bad smell. Jedi Jamal's teammates jubilantly reenact his game-winner, shedding their cold court persona for the more childish one of a spectator. A jar containing crumpled bills sits next to the old man.

"No, hold up! Hold up a second!" Bank is striding towards the bleachers with unclear intentions. The thump of a bass-heavy stereo around the corner inhabits everyone's chest at once. "I'm not the only one here who thinks the result of that game was...questionable—"

"Man, what?" The lean forward's face is comic in disbelief. "You're a funny dude, Bank...the only thing *questionable* was all that fouling you were doing!"

"Please, I got more rebounds than you could in a week!" Bank points his chin in the scorekeeper's direction. "Ask the old timer, he's got the numbers right there…"

Jamal, seated on the aluminum bleachers with a towel around his neck, now rises with a furrowed brow. "So what are you sayin', exactly? Game's over, it's in the books. We all put our money in, and you've been 'round here for a *minute*–you know how it goes." He presses two palms together in mock-praise. "*Please*, enlighten us."

Bank squints his eyes and cranes his head to the side as if to say, "Where do you get the nerve?" He walks slowly up to Jamal until they're almost chest to chest. Jamal, fixed jaw and motionless eyes, meets his gaze with silent fury.

"Enlighten? My uncle is a pastor, I'm taking your sorry squad to church! I already asked God's forgiveness for what's about to happen next…" Bank turns his head to look at the audience for a moment, then resumes the gaze's deadlock. "Three o'clock, same court tomorrow. Winner gets double tonight's pot!"

"Now, hold on just a moment, hot head, I—"

"Easy old timer, we're paying you up front, right now—*double*." The bespectacled grandson grips the scorekeeper's arm anxiously.

"Man, are you serious?" The forward's pointed finger resembles a revolver. "Bank, you're the *sorest* loser I know. We won the game…today! We're taking our money…to-day!"

"Chill, Jake," Jamal commands, his eyes still exchanging daggers with Bank's, "I guess this preacher's nephew needs his sins cleansed or something."

"Jamal, but–"

"We're suiting up tomorrow– I'll see you here."

"Jedi Jamal," a little voice pipes up, "are you going to drop"—the boy scans the paper for confirmation—"16 points, 7 assists, 5 rebounds and… and 3 steals again?"

The smug performer takes a couple steps back, his face spreading into a grin. "You tell me, Stuart Scott!" The scorekeeper gives an ironic snort and looks at Jamal. "Looks like you got a postgame interview, too. I'm not writing *that* down, though!" Some of the players chuckle as they start to pull hoodies and jackets out of their duffel bags. The icy draft that died away a couple minutes ago has once again risen from its grave.

The scorekeeper's eyes are following Bank as the truculent power forward trudges back across the court, to the opposite sideline. The face's wrinkles deepen in recognition.

The names may change, but the players never do.

Chapter Two

The cold city is painted in gray and Noel Gaines has lost his metro pass. The young man's forehead clouds over as he interrogates, one by one, the deep pockets of his dashing twill overcoat—to no avail. Commuters streaming up onto the sidewalk from the subterranean metro sidestep Noel in ritual disdain, some shooting him a glance, that vintage glance native to citydwellers, conveying both annoyance and ridicule. Another fine morning in the nation's capital.

Noel elects to terminate the sorry spectacle in favor of accepting the loss and taking the long walk up Connecticut Ave., through Dupont Circle, up to his flat in Adams Morgan. With a spark of ironic optimism, Noel recalls a chirpy female colleague of his breathlessly reporting, as though she had been searching for an excuse not to live in southern California, that Dupont Circle had been named one of the most "walkable" areas in the country. "Thank God," Noel mutters to himself. He only wishes his errant metro pass was as findable.

Noel begins his trudge up Washington's walkable avenues, teeming Farragut Square the mouth of his journey. Perhaps his loopiness was forgivable, not in a large sense so much as this particular instance, as the late morning found him jumpy with politics, grassroots resistance, and thoughts of his dead father (for whom he had found a song). The new millennium has had no mercy on his soul's intellect.

Mr. Gaines works for a lobbyist, but not one of *those* lobbyists. It's called Patriot Republic, the kind of organization seemingly dispatched on a fool's errand to fight "the powers that be", or, as he sees them, a conglomerated, oversexed, Anglicized Zeus character with credit lines for lightning bolts and a trident made from green, pointy Alexander Hamiltons. Working for a whistleblower in the middle of such a venal regime is like working as a tweed-sleeved shrink for an asylum—there's never an end in sight.

Noel takes part in the fray as an underling to PR's communications director: PR's PR, as it were. (Now inching up the towering beanstalk of Connecticut Ave. towards L St., jostled crosswalks and plotted saplings, the ashen scene sometimes streaked by the bright allure of young women in hip-hugging business skirts.) This week has been all pipe lines, bad trade agreements, and police brutality. Another fine week in the empire.

The voices still run rampant in his head, like children blazing through the rooms of a house after arriving from the bus stop:

> *"This villainous power merger between Nexelon and Epco is not only terrible for sustainability and clean energy, but also threatens the livelihood of DMV homeowners with higher electricity rates."*

> *"This free trade agreement is anything but free trade! It would require a certain masochism on the part of a thinking person to support the deal. The agreement completely benefits the corporate troika and shows no regard for developing countries."*

> *"How many black men will be victimized by the wanton racism of our police force? Why are headlines about another police murder as common as those about car bombs in the Middle East?"*

Noel is almost 30 with light brown skin and brooding hazel eyes. His shoulders are rounded in a faintly robust shape although his participation in athletics could be described as minimal—one of those spoof genetic gifts whose value is lost on the recipient—unlike his late father, Benjamin Gaines, who at one time had a basketball scholarship to Georgetown University in the days of Patrick Ewing. Despite their divergence in activities, the same sharp, close-cropped haircut has adorned both their heads in much the same way.

Smooth,

'Cause I don't get upset-

I pull the plug from the

Microphone then I jet!

Noel chuckles at the sing-songy, rudimentary exultation of an old Rakim lyric, drifting up from his iPhone playlist like the smell of a yellowed book from the attic. Benjamin Gaines, citizen of Chocolate City, had probably relished hip-hop in its early Precambrian stage much as Noel enjoyed the iconoclastic hauteur of Kendrick Lamar today.

Noel was only six when his father stopped coming home from work, but it wasn't until he was seven-and-a-half that Noel fully realized he never would again. Daddy Gaines got into a car accident on the freeway, his mother Penelope had told him. It was when Penelope's chatty aunt from Boston visited two years later that it came out, quite by accident, in one of those domestic breaches of top-secret information that leaves a mother fuming, that, no, Daddy Gaines had been stabbed to death at a nightclub and that was that.

The ides of March in DC offer about as much hope for spring as the Redskins do a championship. Noel clenches his teeth against a new surge of sabre-toothed wind and soldiers on through the homogenous montage of office buildings, their reflecting surfaces mirroring one another in hopes of a dimensional rift. He has his mother's eyes—glassy; full of abstraction; a removed expression. Penelope, her beauty like a peace-treaty between the different races inhabiting her blood, used to dote over Noel like no other: "Here's my extra teaspoon of sugar"—laughing, her fingers tracing young Noel's right cheekbone—"with his father's hair and his momma's eyes!"

Later, Noel would joke that he'd readily trade her eyes if he could inherit her voice in return. Penelope was a fluid mezzo-soprano housed in deep curves when Benjamin Gaines first saw her at a jazz gig over on U St. back in '85. Her skin was of olive, her hair, silk, her voice, pure honey. The fact of her diverse genealogy (black, white, Cherokee) lent Penelope something like a mystical equanimity, as though it gave her communion with the differing secrets of each set of ancestors and thus excused her from going through the motions of mundane life. She drove Benjamin mad.

Benjamin Gaines, as seen in Anacostia, 1985: tall, quite tall, about six feet and three inches, slim and gangly, big hands with the wingspan of a startled gargoyle, chestnut complexion, nicknamed "Showtime" on account of his flair for the flamboyant on the blacktop—he could flash a disarming smile and often carried himself, for reasons we could only guess, as one does after winning an oversized teddy bear for his sweetheart in a game of darts at a nauseating country fair. But for all the organic charm and dandy fit for a headliner, Showtime Gaines was given to the vagaries of frequent mood-swings, that annoying, tag-along twin of genius, and often engaged in a high-speed chase with the fluctuating extremes of his own emotions, a whirlwind which his brooding eyebrows never failed to express.

Though he has long since become another ghost of the nation's capital, many still remember how Showtime rolled out of Dunbar High, a primarily African-American school, with all the pomp and press of a super prep-star ready to cover light-years in a single leap. 31.6 points, 11.2 rebounds, 7.4 assists a game in his senior year and a city title—the numbers were burned into Noel's stat-resistant memory by virtue of an old newspaper clipping pensive Penelope had framed in mahogany. His father's widow still religiously wears Hoyas apparel, poor thing, and this strange condition of loyalty has only increased with age, as Penelope's senility and grace both developed in equal measure.

Noel has gained the fringes of Dupont Circle and weighs the benefits of a cup of coffee against his desire to be home. He is already preparing to pass his favorite kebab restaurant with dramatic regret. By a trick of the gray skies, and those within his heart, Noel's wide-set eyes are a turmoil of green and amber. "Afterwords Café, maybe..." he mouths robotically. The fog on all sides is ever a human fog. Desales St. to M St. to Rhode Island Ave.—Noel can never escape, on such walks, the idea that he has been transformed into a tiny piece, traversing, by roll of the dice, the board of a Monopoly game.

How crazy to think, he muses, that Benjamin Banneker, a black man, reproduced the entire city plan from memory after the volatile L'Enfant had stormed back to France. Our District of Columbia (lumber-columned): statues of white men in the mazes of a black man's mind. Noel recalls with curiosity the black-and-white checkered floors he had seen in some public Masonic lodge, its implied incessancy.

Knowing only fragments of his father's life, Noel feels like simply one more of those fragments, and equally inexplicable. He knows, for example, that Benjamin had dropped out of Georgetown after spending his sophomore year on academic probation, but he doesn't know *why*. He knows, and is now further vindicated by the scorekeeper's existence in knowing it, that Benjamin had become a legend on the playgrounds of DC in some kind of celebrated, infamous street league around the time he met Penelope, but even this means little to Noel.

Not knowing who your father is, he has decided, is the same as working for a duplicitous company who tells you one thing and does another— your whole life (a metaphor formed while working at the office). In her self-absorbed state of mental decline, it isn't like scattered Penelope is in a position to help him, either. His identity is the stuff of papier-mâché, plastered together, easy to fall apart—Noel is half and half, and, without his father, really only half of that.

In sum, the sterile political district of whispered Latin is a world of deprivation in which the line between security and containment is razor-thin. Anything it can offer is merely a means of cajoling our friend into false tranquility. The homeless men with their carts of junk move fluidly between this world and the world of his lost father like renegade organisms who can walk on land as easily as they can breathe underwater. It wouldn't be too alien a world for Noel, no: his cultural lungs could adapt, too. Rather, he has merely shunned what is too personal. As if to shut out the demons of his father's absence, Noel had resolved to build a narrative entirely different from that of Benjamin Gaines. So complete has been his avoidance of the old neighborhood that the idea of it has become akin to a dream-world visible only by a shimmer between waking and sleeping.

When he heard, by dumb coincidence, of the scorekeeper in Anacostia a couple of days ago between the festooned walls of Ben's Chili Bowl, Noel realized he'd rejected his father's world for a far falser one, a place draped in funereal architecture to commemorate its own proudly Roman fate. He slows his stride a bit, lifting either fist to his mouth to warm stiffening fingers.

Finally, the giant round-about of Dupont Circle, like a whirlpool of automobiles. Which caffeinated ventricle of this city is a trustable reality, anyway, if—Noel begins to cough severely. Clouds of exhaust hang heavy. Ah. Yes, that was it—the impressive federal buildings are a network of mausoleums, each interring a fragment of the American vision, much as Buddhist temples in Asia claim to house a strand of hair, no, a toenail of the Enlightened One. The homeless, it seems to Noel, sublime in their gypsy-dark self-entanglement, alone hold the pivotal secret as they shuffle through the grayness measured out in triangulated series of traffic cones.

We gon' be al-right!

Can ya hear me, can ya feel me?

We gon' be al-RIGHT!

Face-numb Noel, having produced his last puff of smoke in the frostbitten air, steps into the wigwam warmth of Afterwords Café. Plainly-dressed

people are standing stationary with heads bowed in the shadow of towering shelves of books which, having seen Noel's approach from the shopfront window, reach out and murmur to him listlessly in the manner of
third-world beggars...*Open me, open me.* Sensible Noel resists the tempta-
tion of trade literature, orders a hot latte, and takes a seat.

The Kendrick Lamar song irks him, tugs at his coattail, exacerbates his
anxiety. *Black lives matter*, voices chanted, *black lives matter*; white fire-
arms chattered, *rat ta tat*, scattered black matter across rainy pavements
in nameless antebellum towns—*black lives matter*, and in mother's room
the news blackly chatters. Each side is vying to occupy Noel's being in an
eternal battle that would make Krishna wince. *We gon' be alright.*

A steaming latte lands with a click on his table. He takes out the chili-
stained napkin (just a bit on the corner) upon which he had made a note
while eavesdropping in the hot air of Ben's Chili Bowl. In the familiar
scrawl of inspiration and bad handwriting, it reads:

**Two guys talking basketball analytics. Unbearably useless num-
ber-crunching. "They're even keeping stats on the playgrounds, and
I'm not talking homicides." What?! Some old man in Dad's hood,
a "one-man Wikipedia". Keeps records on every street-league game
since the eighties. Like some kind of hood savant. Knows my father???
More b-ball drivel.**

Noel quickly folds up the napkin and shoves it in his breast pocket
furtively, like a spy with sensitive intel behind enemy lines. The sudden
movement causes a stir of glances in the café, but the young man's sharp
and strange comportment does little to rouse suspicion, much less hold
anyone's attention. Something unnamable, insistent, instinctive is rising
within his chest, lifting its mass upward with frightening velocity until
just barely, in the range of centimeters, breaking the plane of Noel's sym-
bolistic field: *I have to go back.*

There is suddenly nothing unclear about any of it. Noel drains the cup
of coffee in two gulps, wincing as the hot liquid sears his gullet. His gaze
by default dives down the neckline of an eye-shadowed sorority girl too
absorbed in analysis to know he's there. The young man gets up to leave.

In paying for his latte, he uncovers the rogue metro pass, wedged between dollar bills in the back pocket of his slacks. Noel again directs profanity at his personal failings. "Probably wasn't keeping my eyes to myself", while stealing another peek.

It is a little-known fact that many bookshops, such as this one, have evidently been appointed as official hosts for cosmic accidents, both sensational and banal. In giving the student's soft assets a standard up-down study, Noel notices a flash of color fall from a paying customer's pocket.

"Excuse me," Noel the Samaritan says, walking over, "I think you dropped something."

A bespectacled Asian face confronts him in bewilderment, then jerks its attention to the floor. "Oh!" The foreigner's movements suggest sincere horror in bending to retrieve the item. Noel grins at him good-naturedly and turns to go, sensing the language barrier. The foreigner, however, is now holding the old basketball card in front of him (*Mahmoud Abdul-Rauf, Denver Nuggets*) with a look of great effort contorting his features.

"This, uh…very un-*believable* player. Special card. He…really believe in himself. So, thank you so much!" The address ends on a note of relief, and Noel shakes the extended hand.

Noel is to play the (foreign) exchange back in his mind several times before the day's end. If a moment's impression in the conscious mind was like an uploaded video, this one's views would be sky-high. Was that guy Chinese? Thai? What business would he have in knowing anyone besides an icon, a Michael Jordan? *Mahmoud Abdul-Something*—sounds like a member of the Taliban!

He chuckles out loud. Noel's thoughts are grading back into the fluorescence of those five words (italicized above), his soles stepping outside onto the pavement of someone's black-and-white painting, the pigment still drying and runny, and once again lifting his iPhone's tendrils to either ear he touches, like a blind reader, Kendrick's name; the tunnel of a sidewalk in front of him, thoughts turn to the late Benjamin Gaines, his father (for whom he has found a song).

Chapter Three

Penelope Gaines is on the stage again. Bright lights, gigantic amoeba of a Friday night crowd, swallowing her up with its listening. She is shape-shifting into Carmen McRae in the Black Broadway of U St., her favorite trick, standing in a black satin gown with the olive of her skin aglow, the voice a second voluptuous body sent from her first, flirting, teasing, loosening—the men gasp as she raises with a note her bare right arm. *"I fell in love with you the first time I looked into/Them there eyes..."* Let my voice seize you, lead you, *be* you; let the band behind me undo the lace at the waist of the cosmos as I snap its steady pulse. *Three, four...*

A fierce bulldog glares from the chest of her sporty blue sweater, which hangs loosely off her frail shoulders and tumbles down well past her hips. Without her audience Penelope is an anomaly of grace, aged as she is, moving through her Adams Morgan cubby-hole kitchen as though creating her legacy instead of a microwave lunch. *Benjamin still says I don't belong in this here kitchen.* She had woken up last night and felt herself in his arms again, enveloping her being in warmth, and she knew she wasn't Penelope and he wasn't Benjamin—just two faceless lovers on the same search, as it had been for a millennia. *One, two...*

The woman on stage, now standing in the euphoric aura of applause, is shape-shifting again, becoming older, collapsing to a central point like a folded paper, becoming gray and crumpled. Penelope has caught her reflection in the window. Her braided pigtails hang, like silver stalagmites, around the curve of her still smooth cheekbones and anciently dark doe-eyes. *They said I looked like Eartha Kitt, with them there eyes...Three, four...*

"You are now listening to WPFW 89.9 FM, your member-supported jazz station for the greater Washington area...alright, up next we got some Duke Ellington, 'Take the A-Train'..." Penelope straightens, the half-opened cup of Ramen noodles between her long fingers no longer felt or seen. *If you take the A-Train...you'll find, the quickest way to get to Harlem.* Her voice unfolds like a four-legged thing with wings who forgot how to use them—hoarse, weathered, contained. Something sultry gone a little cold, waiting to be warmed.

...Benjamin! I told you the smell of that dope was too strong, I'm smelling it while I'm singing, man, I swear the whole front row knows I got three doobies in my bra now, baby c'mon..."*I ain't much to look at I ain't nothing to see...I got a man, he's waiting for me...*" Far as I'm concerned that devil of a pianist can wait 'til after the show to get high!...

A collage of scatting concludes the old recording. Duke and his debonair mustache have once again become indistinct, though in her motions they remain as clear as ever, still occupying the bandstand of her attention. In the oven go the Ramen noodles. Penelope's sweeping, glassy eyes settle on the microwave above, whose functionality she now determines to decode. Noel kept telling her to read his instructions in red marker on the fridge's magnet-board, but Penelope was never one for step-by-step instruction.

...Remember, Daddy? You sent me money home every holiday from Puerto Rico with a postcard of tropical beaches and palm trees so pretty and I thought it was funny on Christmas to think of sunscreen and bikinis with a mistletoe over my head and baby Noel in his little sweatpants, and you told me about accounts and trust funds and, well, I told you in my head I'm not *enough* of your daughter to put all that shit together and…well, old Aunt Evelyn ain't in Boston to help me anymore, either!…

Every day Penelope makes love to Benjamin and still smokes a cigarette after. Always off somewhere playing basketball, getting money. Coming home in his big black high-tops and white socks with a numbered navy-blue tank-top. Still laughing some days, still angry others. Yelling and gesturing, glaring at Penelope in fury with those burning brown eyes or kissing her neck and fondly cupping her backside, making her alive, sending fusillades of pleasure and excitement through her feminine canals, all a-flame; forgotten is the long-ago fatality of their bodily fete; fun and games and Funkadelic's "Flashlight" again rule the day.

All the genetic forces within Penelope, her fingers still on the microwave, mobilize and she begins to hum, first quietly and now louder, the unrestrained melody of the song's chorus. Over and over, until it becomes something different—and she does, too.

…I saw you in the cherry blossoms with Noel last April, don't you love how they pop up in the springtime like a magic trick, all pink and moist and Japanese? I knew you loved them, too. I saw you leaned up against one of those twisting little trunks in a grove bursting with color and tenderness, the air was so bright and clear, and you had little pink petals around your feet, hands in the pockets of your overcoat all smiles and laughter, sweetness, love, strength…and Noel said "C'mon Ma, this way! The Dr. King memorial is this way! They sculpted his face and everything, Ma, come on now…." And you know how you and I adore Dr. King, but all I could think about was your lovely face, dark goatee, white teeth, how it was sculpted just for me… Did you smell those blossoms, baby? Did you *smell* them? Like opening a bag of the sweetest candy when you were a child and Grandma had no idea…

The sound of a key in the lock, foretelling a human face. Footsteps, a door slam. The words arrive atop the saddle of a cold, galloping draft. "Hey Ma, it's Noel!" A suspicious pause. "Ma, what's that *smell*? You cooking something?" Benjamin's dark brown eyes had been heated to a fine hazel and now confront Penelope with wonderful concern. The smell of burning plastic makes his head dizzy.

"Jesus, Ma! What you got this cup of noodles in the oven for? You trying to bake a casserole or what?" Noel turns his head to shoot the offender a look. Penelope looks on in saintly rapture—eyes full of abstraction; a removed expression. "You have the microwave on, but the problem is you can't microwave the noodles in the oven!"

A shy giggle. "Now baby…you—you always come in rantin' and ravin' about this or that, acting like you don't know me from the face on the moon! Let Momma Gaines get a look at you…" Sometimes men just work themselves into paroxysms of misdirected virility; you have to soothe them, placate them–

"Momma, hold on a second! You want to burn this apartment down?" Noel rebuffs her advances with fond annoyance. He knows this tone of hers–Penelope's mind hasn't made it to the calendar date, though a conflagration almost has. "Let me take care of lunch for you, OK? I don't know why you don't want to use those directions I put up for you…"

"So stubborn, can't tell you nothing! These men, I tell you…can't tell them nothing. Give them your heart, they say you're tellin' a lie." She abruptly starts humming a tune and eases into her beige dining chair, as though reenacting some premeditated script of discussion. "So pretty, that song. Now Noel, when you gonna take me to see those pretty cherry blossoms again?"

"*Cherry blossoms?* Ma, you know how cold it is outside still? Barely March, means it's still wintertime in Washington. I heard spring might come late this year—"

"Benja—Noel…boy, why do you in-*sist* on bothering your momma today? Huh? Me and your father, we…I told him I'd see him where the cherry blossom trees are *blossoming*. Take me over to the shade, I'll wait for you over there." What kind of lit stage did she imagine herself on, that she kept firing off fragile monologues as though reading lines at a dress rehearsal?

And that smell.

Noel sprays the kitchen with a fruity air-freshener, allowing silence to intervene and punctuate Penelope's curious mania. Even her dementia fit her elegantly. Like a black satin gown no one else had but her. It was all a performance in which everyone besides Penelope played an ancillary role. "I don't know what you…Look, I can take you to the Dr. King memorial if you want, Ma—there's not going to be any cherry blossoms, though. Just people hugged up in their coats breathing clouds. Just wait 'til April, Ma, I promise…"

Here again she speaks with the frankness of a child, giving Noel the maddening suspicion that, somehow, *his* senses are the faltering mechanism. "The people in here come and go to see me," Penelope starts, raising her right index finger while rolling her eyes to the ceiling with a certain affectation. "They always have time, 'cause there ain't no difference between me and them. We stay together, and when I do finally go with them, other people will need for me to come see them, too. Your Daddy and I do ha-…*hanami*—"

"Ha-what? Hammurabi?" Noel is growing more vexed with every word. A familiar vexation, but no less strange and shattering.

"Listen! *Hanami!* He said it rhymes with 'Bob Marley' and Lord knows he probably…he probably did it, too. When the Japanese…see, the Japanese people aren't dummies! They came and sat under the cherry blossom trees, on a pink carpet of the ones that fell…*hanami*. They came in the springtime 'cause they knew that was"– lifting two thin arms high, then slowly bringing them down meaningfully—"the only time those blossoms would come, Noel. Only then! And then"—a finger snap—"they gone, honey. *Hanami.* They gone. And anyone's a *damn* fool if they don't know they're the same!"

The radiator begins its hiss, then rumbles spasmodically. He heard it all the time, but had never quite listened to it until this moment, down to the fine details of its shuddering pipes. A guilt-ridden anger wells up in his own channels. *How could she put me through this?*

"Daddy didn't want my half-and-half ass down in Fayetteville, no sir. Momma was no place, and everywhere. Heard she even fooled around with the KKK just to get her clerk job. Judge Ennis, his friends, all of 'em…no, Daddy sent me up to Boston and Aunt Evelyn quick! Big stinky city, smokestacks…little delis with dirty doors. White schools didn't want me, black schools wouldn't accept me.

"Noel, child…my Aunt Evelyn, God rest her soul! She kept telling me about the cherry blossom festival. Kissing boys, ice cream for some pocket change. Auntie said…Auntie said DC got their first trees in nineteen-oh… nineteen-oh-nine. And burnt them all! All of 'em, Noel! You know why? 'Cause they had *bugs*. Big ol' Japanese ones. When I was a little girl I would cry myself to sleep, and cry, and cry, thinking about that. Who knows why?"

"I don't know, Ma." It's hard to say whether or not Penelope notices his willfully cavalier tone. Noel sets a seasoned bowl of noodles in front of his mother. "Chopsticks?" He gives her a red pair before she can answer. Penelope is gazing into the emerald ceramic bowl as though in the midst of divination, the clouds of steam licking her cherubic face.

"That was the only time Benjamin would be quiet…when we did that *hanami*. And I felt like this great…this great *thing* was opened up tremendously between us, and I could tell him anything, just like I am now with you, honey. Couldn't do that back home, no! He'd fly off the handle when my words were tender, and sensitive…do you understand? Said I might as well not even be on this earth, the way I was talking. Scared him, when I was so far away like that.

"But when we sat under the trees it was different…hell, I was just happy to have dragged him out there, he was such a busy body…and I told him about how I cried when I was a little girl about that, that…that *thought* of burning all them trees, so young and lovely and alive, after having come all that way in a ship 'cross the ocean, just to die like that…and Benjamin would just listen, and smile, and he never acted like that…ha! Never…"

Coltrane's "My Favorite Things" comes on the radio, its effect on Penelope like that of a harlequin figure on a group of schoolchildren in the middle of class. A spiritual levity takes hold of the old songstress, banishing her reminiscence to the place of forgotten things. Lilting saxophone notes stab the air and conversation makes its retreat. Penelope closes her eyes with a deep shudder. McCoy Tyner's piano solo shows her absolutely no mercy, either. "…my fav-orite things-sss," she croaks, rocking back and forth softly.

The Benjamin half of Noel is like a fire spirit whose appearance can only be instigated by flame. Somewhere in his quiet soul, two sticks create friction. *My mother is the curator of a great art gallery who, in the hazy beatitude of her passion and genius, has forgotten how and where to turn the lights on. To compound matters, it is only her gallery that houses the revelatory originals of pieces reproduced carelessly, and thus only through those pale reproductions that the public knows the originals exist at all!* Noel trembles at the injustice of Penelope's state, for not being able to find the lights himself.

"Ma! Well? What about you and Daddy? Aren't you going to tell me more?"

As though a prized vase has shattered in the next room, Penelope's eyes fly open and fix on her son. Her face's serenity is broken by a gale of unhidden alarm. Her mouth slowly moves open and begins to shape sounds, but its voice lags far behind. In the next moment Noel is pressing his palms to his ears, headphones slipping off his neck and dangling to the floor. He has never cringed with more agony.

"Benjamin Lane…Benjamin Lane GAINES…" Fully possessed, Penelope flings her arms wide and nearly pounces on the young man. He catches her in his arms with the first sob, this grieving woman who isn't his mother, but someone's wife, *someone's* wife, holding her heaving, deserted body against his, recoiling at her idea of Noel being…*I don't even know him.*

"Don't ever leave me again, hear? You mean, fucking…unfaithful… *hoodlum*! How can you dare to…to…to *do* me like this? I never hated anything more, loving you…."

The saxophone prattles on about its favorite things, which are many. His only refuge from Penelope's mistaken invective is holding her tighter. Looking over her shoulder to the kitchen table, Noel Gaines realizes that his crazed mother never touched her noodles.

Chapter Four

The scene opens with a pair of ebony-checked Air Force 1s coming into focus, suspended by the shoestrings from a telephone cable. Below is a nameless court off Martin Luther King Ave., Southeast DC, confined by a tall black fence on all sides like forbidden property. Once again, the red and blue teams have taken the court, though the distinction between the two is only made by contrasting shades of gray. While the early afternoon's sun rays have breathed human life into the court, the park's panorama is unwaveringly colorless, even as voices and movement animate the palimpsest. Today the spectators are many, mostly on account of the good weather, and their sharp wit takes center stage as the nonchalant exhibitionism of team warm-ups takes place.

"The Hornets just have bad management, man. You're gonna pay a 38-year old dude 50 million when he's putting more time under the knife than he is on court? C'mon man...I don't care if he's Wilt Chamberlain! Let, the man, GO! He's the past. His hairline is running faster up his head than he can up the court..."

General laughter and hand-slaps ensue.

"It's a young man's game, yo...I swear I saw the homie collecting social security checks during a timeout!"

The speaker dons a tank-top and a bushy goatee, his long dreads wrapped in a well-stretched cap that gives his profile an impressive shape. While his bearing and attire make it plausible that he is, in fact, a seasoned player, it is more likely that he's an established member of the park's color-commentator-by-committee platoon, a sort of rotating cast of front-row Spike Lees who at turns jibe, cheer, jeer, preach, condemn and fling themselves into hysterics in response to the emphatic game action. If it weren't for their incessant narration, glorifying and mythmaking, it is, to put it generously, questionable that any basketball would ever transpire at all.

As the enabling listeners lean on each other for support in spasms of hilarity, a dissenting voice speaks up.

"Come on now, I can't let you disrespect my guy like that. That's just patently *inexcusable*! Twenty years in the league, five rings, two Finals MVPs, an 81-point game—count 'em, 81—," the man pauses for effect with eyebrows arched, an air of professorial dignity passing over his round face, "not to mention...my dude was *clutch*. Game-winners like Mike, cold-blooded. And he did his thing in Rucker Park, showing respect to the legends. Top ten all-time, period!"

"Yeah, whatever man, I'm just done with him," the dreaded jester responds dismissively, "I'm not saying he wasn't great, *in his own time*. He did his thing, no doubt. But there comes a time when you gotta step aside for the young guys who are trying to come up. I remember when he *was* that dude, you know what I'm saying?

"Mike was 40 and on his last legs, and every time the Wizards played the Hornets, your boy let Mike know, 'Hey, it's my time now, old man, why don't you put that baton in my hands?' And we all saw that. I mean, he was 21, 22 dropping 50 all on MJ's head! Same thing now, you did your thing, you got your rings...that 'fro on top of your head done vanished in thin air, time for the young blood to take over...'"

"Yeah? That ain't stopping you from wearing that teal number-eight jersey, though, is it? That's right Casanova, I saw you in Wal-Mart last week with that big-boned girl, come on now..."

An explosive mirth charges through the reclining company of young men, fanning out from the bleachers and reaching some of the players on-court, whose meandering personal dribbles have taken them within earshot. Ridicule is wonderfully contagious in the park.

"It's easy to talk about greatness," a raspy voice suddenly growls, "when you've only seen it from a distance!" Everyone's neck whips around simultaneously in curiosity: the old bearded man on the first row of bleachers is staring back at them, the papers in his lap flaring up at the corners from a light spring breeze. The manifold pounding of basketballs against the pavement is suddenly audible in the young men's ears.

"This generation is blinded by highlight reels! The greatest players and moments were never captured on camera. You think what Michael Jordan did was something? Ha! Give me Connie Hawkins in '64 in a pair of cut-off dungarees on a Brooklyn blacktop, palming that thing like a volleyball and swooping to the hoop with one arm longer than two yard-sticks! Pee Wee Kirkland inventing the crossover right here on the streets—man, can you imagine how far defenders got thrown by a move they'd never *seen* before? It was like Pee Wee brought a light-saber to a knife fight.

"And I won't even talk about the time I saw Jumpin' Jackie Jackson dunk all over Wilt Chamberlain up in Harlem , I mean….we thought Wilt was going to change his name after that one. Kareem changed his name *and* the game, but when he retired he said that Earl Goat Manigault was the greatest to lace up sneakers against him…That dude would fetch a penny off the top of the backboard, brush it off and hand it to you just like that, and I ain't bullshitting you! The *originators*. They'd cross you up with a ball that had three titties on it, I mean…hey! You kids need to listen, this is the history of the game—this old-timer seen everything the game forg—"

"Grandpop, I got your Doritos and diet Coke," a tiny voice interrupts. The scorekeeper's grandson has just popped up, his timing painfully punctual. The scorekeeper clears his throat and nods, haughtily accepting his poison. The scene has a comic effect on our color commentators, who steal ironic looks at one another and stifle laughs. Reverence (or its emulation, at least) is funny that way—it's almost always eager to succumb to the indiscretion of giddy irreverence, if only given the opportunity.

"What kind of basketball has 'three titties', Grandpop? I don't think I've seen those before…" A surge of predictable laughter is interrupted by Jamal, who comes over to inform the scorekeeper that both teams are ready to begin.

The information, which seems commonplace enough at a sporting event, ignites a sudden commotion among the onlookers which, to someone uninitiated in the ways of street hoops, might seem unnerving. In fact, it is merely among the most time-honored traditions of athletics: the placing of bets. Wrinkled dollars clutched in shaking fists punctuate babbled boasts. The effect of such uproar, when seen through a black-and-white, low-resolution lens, comes across as strangely muted, as though it all hadn't quite "undergone the formality of occurring"; coated in a black-and-white veneer, the imagery is disconnected from our experience, and thus assumes the lachrymose quality of a deniable dream.

"I got fifteen on my main man Habeebi puttin' up twenty on you suckers! Hezbollah's Baller, Saddam Insane, The Nicest From ISIS…Habeebi, you feelin' good, right?"

A lanky, floppy-maned Iranian man in markedly higher shorts than everyone else, quietly shooting free throws between his teammates' heaves, looks over, smiles, and flashes a thumbs-up.

"Oh, he's killin' today, he's killin' everything today! Gimme twenty on that fool, let me take your money—that's easy money. *Easy* money! What they call it—an *assassin*. The Persian Assassin, that's your new nickname, Habeebi! You're a national security threat!"

Short and shirtless, one gets the idea that such a young man does sets and sets of push-ups and queer abdominal contortions simply to look all the more impressive in this wild, brash moment of throwing his money away on nothing in particular—or doubling his meager sum only to find himself back at square-one the following day.

A taller figure with frizzy, abating cornrows and an unkempt fu-manchu goatee steps into the fray. His motions are slow and his expression, showing no malignance, has something of an opiated daze across the eyes and sepia-toned cheekbones. "I got thirty bucks on Saint Rod-rigo getting ten rebounds *and* five assists," he says in a drawl.

"Saint Rodrigo! Saint Rodrigo!" they cry in mock adulation, leaning on one another once again for support. "*Fiesta, fiesta…Aye Dios Mio…mucho dinero menana!*" The dreadlocked analyst now runs up to the person in question, pumping his arms in exaggerated haste, and genuflects before the Saint as though he were exalted royalty, bowing with arms spread wide. Saint Rodrigo, who is in fact a young Salvadorian father of two, famous for his savvy, if unspectacular, floor-game, shakes his head and curses them all with a grin.

Of course, "Saint" Rodrigo isn't really a saint, nor is the Iranian small forward, whose real name is Nabil, an assassin or rebel or anything of that sort; the showman Jake doesn't necessarily resemble a snake, nor is Jamal an actual Jedi with misshapen Sith enemies–until they all step on the court, that is. Once they've plunged themselves as before into the breakneck sequences and fleeting one-on-one battles of another scrimmage, on a nameless blacktop in front of the eyes of the neighborhood, blessed with the sunlight's permission, it's as though they've stepped on a stage that requires a special pass and a backlog of credentials, thus transforming them into a class of mythical performers who command a new and greater taxonomy to do justice to their exploits.

And then there's Bank-Shot Davis, whose government name nobody knows.

"To win, or not to win," Bank proclaims theatrically from halfcourt, cupping a ball in his palm and holding it at arm's length, "*that* is the question, my brother! I ain't saying names, but Jamal—oops—and the rest of you teletubbies are still trying to find the answer!"

The scorekeeper snorts and gives Tiresias a sidelong glance. "What you think of that, grandson?"

"I think," the boy says, trying to keep a straight face, "all that trash-talking gives him bad breath."

His grandfather lets out a great laugh, the crow's feet deepening to his temples. He gives Tiresias a warm clap that almost knocks him off the bleacher.

"That's alright son, that's alright...not bad at all! Don't let him hear you say that, 'cause you know—that temper and all. Hey listen, I want you to write those numbers down clear today, you hear? No chicken-scratch, can't have your threes looking like twos and your twos looking like threes! I don't want to have no arguments, no disagreements, no yelling 'cause someone is sure he's losing money on account of our penmanship. You understand?"

"Yes sir", a slightly offended Tiresias responds.

"Nothing to be ashamed of, it's just practice! They came to practice their jump shot, you came to practice your writing, that's all. Here, I want you to try..." The scorekeeper takes the sheet of paper in Tiresias's lap, a graphite grid of names and stat categories with empty spaces for where numbers will soon be, and turns it over to its blank side. "Now I just want you to write three twos, side by side, and then on the next line, three threes in the same way."

The scorekeeper strokes his tangled beard as he watches Tiresias make slow, deliberate strokes, his little face so close to the paper that his nose is almost touching. His mother admitted that his writing had improved, but she hadn't been shy in expressing her misgivings about the boy being indirectly implicated in street betting. It had gotten a little hairy, the scorekeeper reflected, a couple weeks ago when the shooting percentage for a player named Meadowlark Junior had been miswritten, which would have cost several 'enthusiasts' a lot of money had the scorekeeper not intervened.

"How's this, Grandpop?" Tiresias proudly holds up his work, the severity of his concentration diffused into a gap-toothed grin. He's written a series of twos and a series of threes in more or less good form, and followed that up by putting a two and a three next to one another and writing 'Jordan' above the pairing.

"Keep it up, son, keep it up," says the monochrome scorekeeper, "there's no reason you can't write those numbers just like that during game action. Remember, you've heard me say it a million times—*they* put up the numbers, but the numbers are invisible until we take 'em down. Alright? I know you want that Michael Jordan jersey—"

The old man leaves the unfinished thought floating in the warm air—his eyes are trained above Tiresias's head on an approaching figure, unfamiliar yet reminiscent of someone in particular. He walks with the restraint of caution. Everyone in the park senses the alien's presence, keying in on his movements even as they continue their conversations, wagers, strategies and so forth. The man isn't here to play basketball, not in *those* chinos or *that* premium cardigan. Out of nowhere he's strolled into their grayscale afternoon.

"Excuse me, uh…," Noel starts falteringly, "are you…you're—you are the scorekeeper, right?"

"I keep all kinds of scores," the cagey old man responds, "it depends on what kind you're expecting me to keep. If you have some sort of score to *settle*, I can't help you, or they'd call me 'the score-settler'. Not my M.O. These scores"–he indicates the battered blacktop with a casual index finger–"are kept by me, in keeping with my position; the position of scorekeeper, that is. What score that you think I've kept do you want?"

"Well, uh—no, I'm not really sure…I mean to say, you knew my father. You knew him better than me. Benjamin Gaines. That's his name. Benjamin Gaines. He was a basketball player out here in Anacostia. 1985, '86, '87. He went to Dunbar High, got a scholarship to Georgetown, but dropped out. You remember him, right?"

"Benjamin Gaines, Benjamin Gaines..." the scorekeeper mutters to himself, appealing to the sky for swift recollection. He starts to chuckle suddenly, refastening his gaze to Noel's probing face with one eyebrow ironically raised. "Well, I knew you didn't come here to play basketball! What's your name, son?"

"Noel Gaines, nice to meet you, sir," the young man smiles self-consciously, sticking his hand out in belated propriety.

"Well, you staying for the game? We're just starting, should be good... come on man, sit down! Ain't nothing going on here but a little round-ball competition, that's all, a medicine prescribed by the good Doctor Naismith, no side effects! This is my grandson, Tiresias, my understudy..."

Had anyone, Noel wondered to himself, ever prescribed medicine for these projects?

Chapter Five

Though our film maintains its blank, primitive pallor, Noel's subjective vision of the battlefield before him is quite different. While he registers recognizable human movement, his brain finds difficulty in interpreting the various modes of action, almost as though he were looking at a foreign language written phonetically with English letters.

In fact, the rapid salvos of passing, cutting, dribbling, shooting, contesting, and cursing appear in Noel's mind as the pure, ground-zero turmoil of an expressionist piece he'd seen at the National Gallery of Art; the jutting elbows and zoomed-in calf muscles, the pumping neck veins and bulging eyes, the occasional sky-leaps at the lip of the rim, the clash of bodies and their dumb impact, the orchestrated angles on the court that blink phosphorously and guide bursts of speed, all come together raggedly, in Noel's perspective, to form a grotesque composition that is timeless, in the strict sense of physics.

"Nice weather today," Noel ventures, at a loss for words.

"Better than yesterday, at least," the scorekeeper replies without looking at Noel, "you never know in a city like this what the weather's gonna be like. It's warm and sunny in DC, which means it's probably snowing in Maryland with penguins walking around."

"Yeah well, my mother's probably all set to go see the cherry blossoms by now. I keep trying to tell her we have to wait, but she never listens to what I say these days."

The old man glances at him with interest, as though seeing him for the first time.

"In-The-Lane Gaines, that's what we used to call your father. 'Cause he could get in the lane like nobody's business. Kept a quick dribble with long arms, ambidextrous, so he could get past you in a split-second and finish with either hand. In-The-Lane Gaines, goddamn it all...you just had to come and make me feel old today, huh?"

"So you remember him, then? Listen Mister... Scorekeeper—I wanted to ask you something, and it probably sounds strange, but you have to know that I never knew my father, they–they killed him when I was six years old, man. It's a long story, but I don't know the story so I couldn't tell you if I tried. I figured, well, I figured you might have some of those scores from back in the day, specifically February 1987, that's when I was born. I just, you know...maybe I'll find something."

An eruption of noise swallows up Noel's tentative question. Jake the Snake, Jamal's steady teammate, had with one clever move nearly started a riot—racing down the right sideline on a fast-break with two defenders between him and the basket, Jake slowed up and suddenly hurled the ball, with no pretense of shooting, at the backboard. Before anyone could wrinkle their face in disapproval, they realized that the ball had caromed with a single thump to a spot at the free throw line, and now Jake was casually making a jump shot between two stunned defenders.

Noel, having missed the sequence entirely, is slightly alarmed by the uproar. ("The Great White Hope!") The scorekeeper, perhaps sensing his discomfort, locks eyes with Noel and with a half-smile shakes his head. He starts to talk through the buzzing noise.

"I've heard your father's story many times. I didn't know In-The-Lane—you said Benjamin?—Benjamin that well himself, but I know the story. I can tell you he tore up these Anacostia parks though. I'll never forget that title game between the Squires and Eagles, let me tell you. See, this is the Kings League, and back then things were different. Back in those days, the Kings League featured cross-city championships. Now it's just here in Anacostia. Anyway, there were hundreds and hundreds of people crowded in that park, and it was hot as the devil that afternoon.

"Your Daddy was a *bad* sucker, let me tell you. He looked like Dr. J. You know Dr. J? Julius Erving. Streetball icon way before his NBA career. And Mr. Gaines was just like him. Came down the court one time, three guys trying to beat him to the hoop, and when he jumped it was like his arms opened up into wings—he cuffed the ball in midair, swung it one way, swung it the other, and BOOM! On all three of their heads. People made such a commotion the cops showed up, and we had to stop the game for about 30 minutes just to restore order. It was beautiful, son. That's when the game was pure."

"What do you mean when you say you know his story?"

"Well, it's just tough out here, you have to understand that. I've seen a lot of guys dragged into the street life, so deep they could never get out, even when they had God's name dripping off their lips. When it comes to drugs, cocaine, all that—nothing's changed but the prices. Crack hit DC hard, you know that don't you? Lotta souls never escaped the Reagan years.

"Look at Pee Wee Kirkland, they don't call him a legend in two games for nothing. And he played ball down there at Norfolk back in the day; he changed what it meant to have a "handle". But he was handling way more than Naismith leather, let me tell you. Made lots of money in the *other* game, went to prison. And he's lucky. If your daddy got killed in these streets like you say, it wasn't for no reason. Sometimes I think hustlin' just means pressing the fast-forward button on your life…you reach the end too quick."

A soft ripple quivers across the scene, almost indistinctly, and suddenly the interlocking motions of the game are suffused with dull tones, mostly beige, but semblance of color nonetheless, and slowly, muted greens, yellows, oranges focus into existence, splashing the seamed rims of t-shirt sleeves, the ridged panels on the surface of pivoting sneakers. The introduction of color onto the dimensionality of the frame resembles a kind of awakening wherein the watcher's perception is finally allowed through the gates of visual acuity. The reds and oranges dimly glare, the blues and greens caress and cool, and millions of microscopic reeds now sway with uniform elegance in the retina.

The game is one of those brutal affairs where made baskets are sparse and each possession is treated with growing desperation. This recognition, that the contest won't be won by a shooter's touch but rather sheer, exacting determination, makes every loose ball like a gleaming nugget in the California gold rush, often resulting in collisions and ending in vicious scrums somewhere between the free-throw line and halfcourt.

Tempers are escalating, blood is running hot. Trash-talk is beginning to reach new heights as an art form. Noel smirks to himself—in the city of Washington, it isn't surprising to see people with little difference in personal motive don red on one side and blue on the other. Even he, however, can't help but be amazed with the efforts of little Tiresias, whom the scorekeeper has allowed to take over officiating for the day in addition to his duties as statistician.

Noel is at once quieted by the elder's queer statements and growing more curious about the nature of this strange league that his father, "In-The-Lane", had at one time passed through the revolving doors of. The longer the game goes on, the more unlikely the whole arrangement seems to him.

"So you said this is called the Kings League, right?"

"That's right."

"Well, how does it work, exactly? Is it like a professional street league?"

The scorekeeper chuckles as he watches Jamal finally rip a jumper from the left elbow.

"You don't come around these parts much, do you?"

Noel affirms with a shrug and remains silent.

"Well, the Kings League was started back in the 70s. Basketball was more popular than ever in the inner cities and projects; it brought the community together and cut some of the gang violence down. Some people had the idea they could make money out there, started selling hot dogs, hamburgers, that sort of thing. That's when the Mob came in—yes, the Mob. That was their heyday. They said, hey, why don't we make a league for the ghettos and make some money off bets, like the horse races?

"And that's just what they did—organized twelve teams in the greater metro area, had rosters, jerseys, logos, everything. The whole nine. Even brought coaches in for some of the games—I remember seeing ABA scouts in the stands holding them American-flag balls, ready to sign guys. And the Mob needed scorekeepers so they could bet on more than just the winner, you understand? Game statistics, points, rebounds…I was homeless back then, but they said they'd pay me a percentage. They heard I was a math prodigy, which was half true. And there we were."

Noel's mouth is half open. "So this is all one big Mafia operation?"

"Oh no-no-no," the scorekeeper says with a grimace, "they got cleared out a long time ago."

"So…?"

"So when the feds cracked down on them in the late 80s, early 90s, the Kings League fell through. The money wasn't there anymore for promoting and organizing. But you know what? Fellas still wanted to hoop, that was never gonna change. So me and a gentleman by the name of Cottonwood Jones, rest in peace, took matters into our hands—at least for Anacostia. We said no more cross-city competition, let's just keep it east of the river. We've always had ballers out here, and back when they were doing the cross-city thing a lot of guys had to be cut 'cause they were doing 10-man rosters. Not anymore. We pooled some money together, got jerseys made up, and set our price for keeping score at a basic level—we made our own league...we *remade* the Kings League.

"And I've been scorekeeping for these boys out here ever since. They're playing for money, for notoriety, and at the end they give me a cut for keeping their stats. It's bragging rights, you see? No more bookies out here, either, no more loansharking. That was the Mob era. Cats can make bets with whomever they want. That's something you have to understand, son. As long as there's a game to be watched, people are gonna find a way to make money out of it. These courts, to me, are like one big piece of paper—they get written on, erased, written on again. And I'll tell you, that's something changeless."

Bank, clad in powder blue, is at center court with both arms raised in the air, looking at the scorekeeper with a victim's disbelief in response to a Tiresias ruling. "Keep it moving, big baby," the old man warns. Bank delivers a knockout punch to the air in frustration and turns to get back on defense. "Go back to Africa, Manute Bol!" drunkenly calls one of the color commentators from behind Noel.

"I see," sighs a disconcerted Noel, "well, would you still have any of those scores from when my dad was playing, by any chance?"

"We've got them at the house," interjects Tiresias, "you can come over for dinner and look at them!"

"Well hold on now, little man," the scorekeeper grins, "your mother won't take to us having a guest without telling her first, I know that much!"

Noel finds himself getting up to leave, although he'd planned on staying for longer. "I've gotta catch the green line soon anyway, don't worry about it. Maybe another time. I—I really appreciate what you've told me though, Mister..."

"Anderson! Marshall Anderson. That's my real name son. Seems like everyone goes by nicknames out here–like a bunch of movie characters, and maybe that's all we'll ever be. Your father was a legend back in the day! There are folks still out here who remember him—even if you don't. He's a part of this place, and now so are you."

But, as Noel strolls alone back down the sideline with a game raging at his back, he couldn't disagree more. He's never felt more ridiculous than he does in this moment precisely because he had no business being there, and further, he feels embarrassed to remember that naïve hopefulness with which he had gotten off the metro in Anacostia, Kendrick Lamar exhorting him in either earbud. Joyless faces follow him for interminable seconds, their fingers spreading into the chain-link fence as though rooted there. *Why are you here? You don't belong here.*

The scorekeeper's words have left Noel with a desolate, empty feeling for reasons he is too numb to analyze. Like the horse races, he had said. *Like the horse races.* As if they were all beasts kept in stables whose spirits were only sanctioned to show life when it was time to make criminals a quick buck. But even here, Noel feels cast out—how could he relate to something like that?

I'm fucked up

Homie you fucked up

But if God got us

We gon' be al-RIGHT!

Noel turns out onto Martin Luther King Jr. Avenue and starts walking up the street in the direction of the metro station. The brightness of newly built businesses, shops and boutiques lining the sidewalks looks tacky in comparison to the historical houses preserved from the 19th century, whose sagging porches and general deterioration give Noel a sense of the place's depth. His eyesight darkens.

A thousand black faces crowd into his mind, distraught, defiant, at first asking which land is theirs, and now growing restless they demand to see Freddie Gray—shop windows shatter; a liquor bottle splinters into a thousand pieces on a street corner; bullets sing through a sunny afternoon; eyes look downward behind a black mourning veil; beads of sweat trail temples in the Selma heat; a thousand hands stretching, stretching to graze Noel's fingertips.

Suddenly, they all withdraw at once and Noel sees a middle-aged man with fair brown skin and curly hair beneath a tan beret approaching him on the sidewalk. The man is wearing a navy-blue basketball jersey with "Nuggets" written in gold across the chest, a stylized number three trimmed in red beneath it. Noel is smitten with deja-vu. Where have I seen that before? I know it from somewhere, but why would I recognize—and then a series of pictures from the previous day parade before him: his metro pass, a coffee mug's click, the undergrad's diving neckline…and a determined face.

"Excuse me, is that a Mahmoud Abdul-Rauf jersey, by any chance?"

The man stops and raises his eyebrows. "Why yes it is—wow man, you know your stuff. It takes a real NBA fan to know Abdul-Rauf." He suddenly looks with puzzlement in the direction of the park. "I haven't missed that game, have I?"

Noel laughs with sincerity for the first time all day. "Not at all, they're still playing, don't worry. I'm actually not a basketball guy at all. I just… keep seeing this guy pop up lately, that's all. He was Muslim, wasn't he?"

The man has a congenial face with a crescent moon of wiry fuzz creeping up his chin, a not unpleasant hint of portliness to his frame. His voice has a nice timbre to it—not the tonality of a singer's, but rather of a man who's constantly used it to express ideas. As he prepares to answer, the older gentleman clasps his hands behind his back, apparently relishing the chance to talk on the subject.

"You're right, he was a converted Muslim. He was born as Chris Jackson and became a Muslim in the 90s. Now, Mahmoud is the all-time leader in free throw percentage, only he's not recognized as such because he didn't have enough attempts to qualify. You see, Mahmoud stopped standing for the national anthem before games because he didn't think that America's political values were in line with his Islamic beliefs. And if he wore Nikes in a game, he'd cover up their logo. It wasn't long before Mahmoud was out of the league, and if you ask me and a lot of the Muslim community, it had nothing to do with his basketball abilities."

"Yeah, I can see what you mean," says Noel, scratching his chin, "so you're Muslim, then?"

"Burak Abdul-Hafiz," the smiling man affirms with extended hand, "that's Bu-rak—not like the president."

When Noel introduces himself, however, Burak's features at once submit to an expression of wonder, his eyes widen, and he clutches the brim of his beret in disbelief.

"*Noel...*why, you're Ben Lane Gaines' son, aren't you?"

It's now the younger man's turn for puzzlement. "Yeah...?"

"All praise to Allah! Do you know that your father and I were fast friends back in the day? Man, we were inseparable for a time! I was the only guy he'd allow to be his point guard...not because I was so great or anything, just because I knew exactly where he wanted the ball, and when, too. Man...and to think, you're the one who stopped *me* on the street! That's the way things work in God's world, though. Listen—"

A cry of anguish and pain rises up from the park behind them followed by a rant of severe cursing, immediately silencing Burak and catching his attention. He turns back to Noel with troubled eyes.

"I think my son hurt himself again out there," he says, shaking his head, "I'd better go check on him. Noel, I can't tell you how overjoyed I am to see you here after all these years. Let me give you my card...are you free this Thursday evening? We live right over here in the historic district. I'd love to have you over, man, in-shallah, to catch up and hear what you've been doing, and your mother, she's still…?"

"Yeah she's still here with us, though who knows for how long. It's strange, but I think you're the reason I came out here. We're up in Adams Morgan—I can take the metro, no problem. I mean, you really mean it?"

"With all my heart, young man," Burak exclaims, now beginning his parting steps while still facing Noel, "Anacostia ain't that bad, you know. We stay in a nice little townhouse not far from here. Still, it's funny how every city's M.L.K. Ave. is the shadiest, isn't it? Give me a call!"

Noel gazes at the retreating figure, "Abdul-Rauf" spelled in white on his back, and then looks down at the card in his hand. *Burak Abdul-Hafiz, Sociology Professor at Howard University.* Noel shakes his head in disbelief, mutters something to himself, and slowly begins to walk up the street with clear eyes.

A saintly city sky is beginning its gradual surrender to twilight; the air cools in its new appointment as night-messenger. The colors of this dull, commonplace road have sharpened to a degree that calls in amazement. Technicolor, in comparison, is almost hyperbolic in its flaring presentation of shade and hue, the stuff of cartoons. No, the lens has once again adjusted, and now the blank avenue is pictured simply as it *is*. The texture of asphalt is set off by a darkening blue sky and the bursting yellow of a closing shopfront. The act of seeing becomes a conveyance. For the viewer, it's as though a hand had turned a tuning knob clockwise—and *voila*!

Chapter Six

Noel has just a moment ago entered the home of Burak Abdul-Hafiz, tracking in snow on the dark oak wood floors. His second sally into Anacostia has been markedly different today if for no other reason than the weather. Mercurial as Penelope's moods, the Mid-Atlantic climate is always a mess around the ides of March. A fresh six inches of snow had descended like a thief upon the nation's capital in the wee hours of the morning, following a sharp cold front that had everyone reluctantly tucking shorts and skirts back in their closets, dreams of spring along with them.

The meteorologists were in top form all morning, foretelling disaster for the highways as though it were a source of special glee. Commuters huddled together reluctantly for warmth throughout the capital's metro stops, waiting grimly for the silver zephyr of the next train. Only Noel's coursing anticipation of his meeting with Burak could counter the mean chill's tightening fingers. His impatient evening walk into historic Anacostia found dove-white snow on the roofs, trodden snow sullied brown on the curbs, and defiantly greenless birch trees that spread like a grin through the gray air.

The address in his gloved hands had led him into the heart of the historical district, and Noel soon found himself approaching a multicolored, street-long row of Italianate townhouses whose playful pastels projected a saddened whimsy from their twilit cloaks of ice. The figures in his palm left him standing in front of the one with a cream-trimmed green façade. A railed front porch with its beveled little roof suggested warmer days of sweating lemonade pitchers and friendly tobacco smoke rising up past the cream slanting eaves. As though stepping into a forgotten corner of history, Noel gingerly scaled the three little stairs and stepped onto the porch with uncertainty. The door was swinging open and there stood Burak, cursing the cold and ushering his visitor in with laughing eyes.

The interior of Burak Abdul-Hafiz's townhome, by most estimates around 150 years of age, is a sight to behold. The floors, as mentioned, are of a heavy oak and its panels creak deeply as Noel and Burak make their way to the parlor couches, while looking up one notices cedar wood beams running from one end of the high ceiling to the other. A thick, refinished balustrade lines a staircase that begins just beyond the front door so that, following the host, we are led to our right into a carpeted space with a delicate glass coffee-table around which Burak and Noel are now taking a seat.

The eye is first drawn, however, to a sprawling painting of an Islamic mosaic, perhaps of Cordoban origin, positioned above the couches like a beacon, and secondly to a bookcase that extends over a third of the room's wall and stands about six feet in height. An old, drafty odor permeates the townhouse, as if history itself were still breathing.

The two men exchange pleasantries and commiserate about Washington's miserable cold spells, which reminds the beaming host to take his guest's coat, with a show of charming embarrassment, and drape it over the balustrade. Burak, Noel notices, is today dressed more like an academic than when he met him on the street, with a denim collar peeking out at the neck from a dark green sweater, a nifty pair of reading glasses angling down his nose, and a brown kufi atop his head that crowns his stout figure with distinction. It's terribly easy to come under the influence of Burak's personality, as his manner of talking seems to impress one with the belief that he's been invited into a small circle of confidentiality. Most of Burak's social quirks can be interpreted as varying forms of scriptural meekness, as though the Koran itself could be interpreted through his facial expressions.

A residual smile still on his lips, something above the kitchen door-frame catches Noel's eye. He is immediately drawn into its center, where a jet-black pupil seems to hold his gaze and read his thoughts like a data-chip. The pupil is encased in a fractal set of sequentially expanding circles, some different shades of blue, others white.

"What is that up there?" asks Noel, pointing a finger.

"Ah! You have a good eye, young man—and I say that deliberately. In Turkey it's known as the *nazar*. The *nazar* is a protection against what we call the evil eye, *Isabat' al-Ayn,* or the power of any entity, visible or otherwise, to infect us with tribulation or bring us harm. Which means, obviously, you wouldn't be here unless you did have a good eye! Some folks get it twisted and think this *is* the evil eye, and I always tell 'em to just—"

"Turn on CBS, and you'll get the strange feeling you're being watched," enunciates a voice from the staircase. "That's his favorite line right there!"

Jamal is slowly making his way down the stairs, clutching the balustrade with his left hand while a set of crutches protrude from the crook of his right arm. A black, clasped brace can be seen on his right knee, just under the edge of his gym shorts. His joke's smugness is mixed in to the grimace on his face.

"Careful, son! You need some help? Come sit down with my man Noel here. Noel, this is my son Jamal. You saw each other at the court the other day, right?"

Both young men nod somewhat curtly.

"Turns out Jedi Jamal here took a blow to his knee while we were chattin' on the sidewalk. Just a Type 2 sprain though, huh Jamal?"

Jamal hobbles over to Noel and shakes his hand, their eyes meeting briefly for the first time. Their curiosity in one another is mutual, but like most young city men, that curiosity is muzzled by the studied distance the city teaches young men to keep between one another, like schoolboys dressed up in an elaborate armor of masculinity.

"Any better this evening?" queries Burak, stroking his wiry goatee.

"Not yet, Pop," replies his son, plunking down on a couch with his knee straight as a board, "Doesn't sting as much as a couple days ago, but... if you're talking about my anger at that filthy animal who calls himself a basketball player, well, nothing's changed..."

"Balance, son, balance. There's nothing that's going to come from that anger; there's nothing that's going to come from allowing it to be a guest in your house. Remember what I said: anger is like being in battle and turning the sword on yourself. Take refuge from it!"

Jamal exhales dismally and glances at Noel.

"I know you saw him out there, right? That dude named Bank? Well...it was a tough game, both sides scrappin' for everything, and that's when ol' Bank likes to get dirty. I went up for a shot at the rim, high in the air, and he shoved me down so that my kneecap"—Jamal pounds an open palm with his fist—"hit the pavement at full force. Doctor said I need to chill for a couple months, at least..."

"I think I know who you mean," reflects Noel, "the big chunky super-villain guy, right?"

Jamal gives a hoot of delight, his face opening into a grin for the first time that evening. "The big chunky super-villain guy, exactly! Hear that, Pop? I con—what's that word? I con-*cur*."

"Don't look at me," counsels Burak, "ask Mr. Gaines over here. He's the one working in the shadow of Capitol Hill! That's some kind of career you got going for yourself, son—your father sure would be proud."

"I appreciate that," Noel says with gratitude.

"In fact, my superstar son over here is in much the same position that your father was years ago. Jamal has all the talent in the world, but he's also a young knucklehead that lets the streets go to his brain. You see, I don't know how much you know about Islam, Noel, but the Prophet Muhammad–praised be his name—taught the Arab tribes that learning and education were *necessary* for anyone who wished to be a serious Muslim and dedicate his life to Allah, the most high. 'He who leaveth home in search of knowledge, walk in the path of God.' So if we can get you into that community college, Jamal, that's a start. Take this latest experience with the Kings League as a sign."

"The Kings League has made me better, though," replies Jamal, rolling his head to the side and turning the corners of his lips up in customary exasperation. Noel, sifting through the conversation with a growing anxiety that won't be overcome, notices that both Jamal and his father share the same open, sensitive eyes, the same waxing-moon forehead, a similar posture around the shoulders—even their legs are both crossed at the ankles, which both father and son are identically oblivious to.

"Which I'm glad to hear," says Burak, "because now's the time to move on from that scandalous abomination of a basketball league. You've been playing with fire long enough; it's time start a new chapter. There aren't any hoop dreams that are worth your life, boy." The professor of humanities turns to the riveted Noel. "They certainly weren't worth your father's life," he says softly.

"You're talking about the Kings League, right? How—I mean, I talked to that scorekeeper over there during Jamal's game. Marshall Anderson. He told me that the Maf-" Noel stops himself, the word half-spoken on his open lips. The force of realization has robbed him of speech. "The Mafia...you don't mean to say...?"

"God's blessings be upon you," sighs Burak after a pause. The professor removes his glasses to wipe them with a cloth, staring at the copper filigree swooping around his feet on the red carpet. Collecting himself,

Burak restores the dainty glasses to their perch on his nose and first raises his hands in an explanatory gesture, as though by doing so the appropriate words will be summoned. "I don't know what he told you, but Marshall Anderson has seen some things. Jamal doesn't like to hear this, but it's the truth. Ol' Marshall never killed anybody, but he never spoke up or tried to change anything, either. Now I don't know how it stands today, but the Kings League was never anything more than a betting and money laundering racket ran by some of the Gambino families in New York. Did he tell you that?"

"Well, sort of…he just said it was started by the mob for the community or something back in the day, but that when the feds cracked down on organized crime he and his friend, uh…Cottonwood—"

"Cottonwood Jones," Burak interjects with disdain. "Man, that ol' score-keeper really gave you some rhetoric, didn't he? When the feds, like you said, started playing hardball with the mob bosses, they did take a major hit. But not only did they still have goons on the street that detectives couldn't track down, they also had black proxies. We used to call them 'scarecrows' because they were propped up, you see, and they didn't have any more power than what their handlers gave them. The mob was desperate, so they had to do something they'd never really done before: employ black men.

"Cottonwood was one of those scarecrows, and whether Mr. Anderson will admit it or not, he was too. They only dissolved the Kings League the first time so that when your scorekeeper showed up again 'for the community', teams were now willing to pay for his box scores up front, and he still got a percentage of any bet that was stat-based. All that goes to the mob and they gave the scarecrows just enough to keep 'em going."

"Who killed him, then?" The words escape Noel before he sees them coming.

"The bets," Jamal suddenly speaks up, "the bets killed him."

"But—"

"Well, there's more than that, Jamal. As I said before Ben Lane Gaines and I were close, and I felt his own sufferings like they were my own. *Bismillah*...He never recovered from the disappointment at Georgetown. When he met Penelope he had everything in front of him, and so did she. But when Benjamin dropped out I saw a man spiraling towards his own destruction, and he was taking Penelope with him. Your mother is an amazing woman, Noel. I know for a fact that she saved his life on several occasions, in her own way. But Benjamin had already exiled his soul to the isles of self-mortification, and she knew it.

"I couldn't bear to see all that talent and capacity get so twisted up and mangled, man, I mean...one moment he was attracting big-time university scouts with his jump shot, the next he was serving the lotus-eaters just up the street here with a nine-millimeter in his pocket. One time I ran into Ben at the courts, sometime in '91 or '92, he took me to the side and said, 'Hey man, you wanna know something crazy? I know I'm gonna die doing what I'm doing, but that doesn't stop me from doing it! What does that make me?' I didn't have an answer for him, and that question still haunts me to this day."

"So you're saying he was suicidal?"

"When you're a nihilist like that, your eventual death is something your actions become obsessed with. Hopelessness, man. When a man feels like he's missed his chance, he feels as though nothing matters, and his perception of personal value lost is converted into a devil-may-care recklessness. If suicide is a kind of marriage, then your father was a perpetual flirt. But, but...Ben, you know...he saw a lot of redemption in you, son. It was just that he was too far gone to change his ways. Basketball was his only solace. I watched him improve on the court even as his life fell apart, even as Penelope threatened to leave—stop me, Noel, if what I'm saying is too much! I'll give you the true story until you tell me otherwise!

"Anyway, they called him 'Showtime', they called him 'In The Lane Gaines', I mean...he was a star in every park he stepped in. A street icon. His teams owned the Kings League—Benjamin knew how to make his teammates better, too. So the bookies started going to him, and the book-ies told Ben they'd pay him off to score less points. Why did they want to do that, you might ask. Well, the smart money was on Ben Gaines' team winning by 20. If you come out and say 'I bet they only win by 5', then you got yourself some bets. And if you've paid off the star player, you're looking at a huge pay-day. But when the bookies came knocking, your father said 'no'."

None of the three men speak for several seconds as the words of Burak sink in. The transom above the front door is darkening; voices rise and fall from the street as another evening ebbs into the old house's memory. Noel fancies that the house itself trembles from the amassed pressure of all the things it holds on to, the age-old dreams and scenes captured in dead wood, longing to be told, shown and talked about. The bookcase stands impressively, remotely, woven with authoritative silence. Titles like *The Tenets of Sufiism* or *The Book of Healing by Avicenna* appear to Noel like momentary wave-crests rising from a greater sea of anonymity, impossible to recall one by one but contributing to a larger feeling of unsolicited grace. Burak pulls the chain on a table lamp and clears his throat.

"Benjamin was the one who got me into Islam, you know. It was like he began fueling the flames of his own demolition with flammable ideas, any sort of provocative notion that could at once save his soul and make all his fury mean something. Ben was resigned to burning out, but he became fixated on burning out *righteously*. He came under the spell of the Five-Percenter heresy, the Nation of Islam—started passing out pam-phlets to guys after games and talked about how the white man was the devil. I always regretted that I couldn't express the great peace I found in the Quran to him sooner, the pure solace of Allah—"

He directs an open palm to the Moorish mosaic above Noel's head, a swirling complexity of spherical blues and reds, like a living cell under the spell of holy music.

"But those were the times of Rodney King and the race riots in Los Ange-les, Ice Cube and N.W.A., raised billysticks and black neighborhoods burning into the night. Everybody was angry, man. Everyone had *had* it. Ben started to feed of that energy, it was like he could barely contain himself. He was just waiting for his chance to make a stand.

"Those bookies gave it to him, man. He didn't need to think twice about it. I think in Ben's mind he was channeling the civil rights days, standing up to the white establishment and all that. He wanted to be a martyr for the cause and go out swinging. It didn't matter who those bookies were, or who the mob guys were. In Ben's world, they may as well have been the ol' governor George Wallace and a bribed Senate all over again, living off black oppression and demanding that he dance the Sambo dance. He did the opposite and dominated that game to the point where those thugs had no choice but to…well, I think you understand…"

Noel Gaines nods his head slowly and sighs, trying to form the sentence out loud that he's wanted to for so long, that Burak has already read in the turning hazel of his eyes. Jamal stares intently at Noel with quiet fascination, his new phone untouched on the coffee table.

"For as long as I can remember, I've always felt, like, racially schizophrenic…you know? But I never knew my father, so it's like in some ways my life has been unoccupied by blackness, or like there's an important door in myself that I can't open. Mama's father and his family always helped us out financially from a distance, put me through school…our life has been the life of white privilege, actually. But I never fit in with that crowd, either. I've never known wholeness, I just exist in separate pieces that don't have any relation to one another.

"My moods are like two roommates who are always at odds, but they have no choice but to live in the same house. All that stuff you're talking about—civil rights, Rodney King, oppression—I know about it, but I don't really *know* about it. See, then I'll put myself on trial for ignorance. All the stuff with police brutality and the Baltimore protests… it's like I'm looking through a glass wall with a perfect view, but I'm prevented from… *feeling* any of it. Sometimes I think my confusion is just the relic of how confused my mother and father were when they got together–"

"May Allah grant you peace, Noel," Burak interrupts suddenly, "if only you knew the great love that existed between your mother and father, and still does! You know what I remember about Ben's last game up the street here? He had taken a black marker and written on his sneakers his initials and Penelope's, 'BG' and 'PG', kind of like how you see lovers carve their initials into the bark of trees. I don't recall him ever having done that before. I'll tell you, it was something to see how those two were so irresistibly drawn to one another, just like the famous Persian poem of Layli and Majnun, 'the mad one'. That's who they were. When I think about Benjamin's early death, it only highlights for me that you, Noel, were an *irresistible* occurrence."

Penelope's painful ravings play themselves over in his head like an old tape, the extremity of her upturned expressions, crazed gesturing, gut-wrenching wails—how tightly she held Noel in that moment of need with a Hoya bulldog across her chest, the chords in the Coltrane song beating a sunny trail to infinity.

"Hey Pop," Jamal breaks in, "aren't you going to show him that paper we have?"

"Ah! Almost slipped my mind…Noel, I've kept something as a keepsake from that legendary game of your father's. I managed to get a copy from Anderson, don't ask how…" Burak Abdul-Hafiz is rummaging through a stack of magazines on the lampstand, pushing his glasses up the bridge of his nose. Jamal makes eye contact with Noel and, lifting himself up slightly, reaches his hand out to Noel. "I'm glad we met, man," he says as their hands clasp in a firm handshake. "I'll have to get your number before you leave. I won't be doing much of anything these next couple of months," Jamal adds, looking bitterly at the cast on his knee. The young men share a laugh.

"Alright Noel," Burak interjects, "check this out!" The professor passes his pupil a white sheet of paper in protective laminate, a smile playing on his face. "I think you found the scorekeeper you were looking for."

Noel's eyes rove the scrawled box score hungrily, following the column of incidental names down, down until he falls upon the prized one: *Showtime*

Gaines. His heart fluttering, he follows the row across into the numbers, which stand like monuments. *52 points...14 rebounds...6 assists...6 blocks.* Noel takes a deep breath as the numbers come alive and speak his father's pyrrhic masterpiece. He now finds himself inhaling the moisture of young cherry blossoms as if he were in a sunlit grove full of them—despite the fact it still isn't April, and that Washington yet lies under a thick carpet of ice.

About the Author

Julian Mihdi is a graduate of George Mason University with a bachelor's degree in English and also holds a TEFL certificate as an ESL teacher. Born in South Carolina and raised in Virginia by a literary family, Julian received much of his inspiration for *Chimera* while living, traveling and teaching English in Southeast Asia for nearly four years. He is also the author of the
2016 e-book *How To Be A Successful ESL Teacher*. Currently based out of Salt Lake City, Julian plans to continue to travel the world and publish as many books as possible. You can follow his exploits, read his articles and browse some of his previous travel writing at his website, www.julianmihdi.com.

Made in the USA
Lexington, KY
21 April 2017